Yesterday Tomorrows
The Dark Secret

Denise Buckley

Strategic Book Publishing and Rights Co.

Copyright 2012
All rights reserved — Denise Buckley

No part of this book may be reproduced or transmitted in any form or by any means, graphic, electronic, or mechanical, including photocopying, recording, taping, or by any information storage retrieval system, without the permission, in writing, from the publisher.

Strategic Book Publishing and Rights Co.
12620 FM 1960, Suite A4-507
Houston, TX 77065
www.sbpra.com

ISBN: 978-1-61897-361-0

Typography and page composition by J. K. Eckert & Company

With thanks to Reg, my husband,
my family,
and my writer colleagues
for their help and patience.

T*he* S*tory:*

Ruth loves Billy but should she accept his proposal of marriage? She always wanted children but now he's returned from WW1 after being shot, and is unable to give her the children she wants. There is another man in her life, Alfred. Who does she choose?

To add to the confusion, Uncle George is making life difficult for her. Her problems continue to grow especially when she finds herself pregnant. She must put on a brave face and battle through. What's more, who murdered the gentleman living in the mansion and threw the knife in the river where Billy found it? Did they know him?

These are the problems Ruth must face and try to resolve.

My story is set in Dukinfield, Cheshire, UK, a mill town, in the early 1900's. The characters are all fictional and the story tells of what life was like then, when there were no jobs and never enough money.

Chapter 1

What's that? I stiffened—listening. The sound of crackling disturbed me and my chest felt on fire. Was it a nightmare? I'm eight years old and I have never wakened to that noise before. I opened my eyes. There was smoke swirling around me. My eyes began to sting. The baby, Mary, whimpered in her drawer beside me. This was no nightmare; it was real; really real. I heard my mam scream from upstairs.

Crash! Part of the ceiling came down and spat out sparks and fire into the room. I attempted to shout but I had no voice. I threw the coat on one side that covered me. My throat felt dry and my eyes burned as I stood up. I can't see anything but smoke. Bending over I felt for Mary, and touched her face. My Mam's old dress that I wore was in the way. I picked Mary up, tucked her under my right arm and pulling my dress up, I pushed it into my right hand, keeping my left hand free I felt my way to the door.

It was hot, very hot and I struggled to hold Mary as my fingers fumbled around. I touched the window and moved my hand over the wall searching for the door. I cried. I could taste the smoke. It filled and blocked my nose!

Mary whimpered and her small body flopped about like a rag doll. She was slipping. I felt dizzy as I pulled her closer to me. There wasn't time. I squealed in terror. There were voices coming from outside but there was fire all around us and I was getting very tired. I felt Mary slipping again from my grasp so I managed to cling hold of her vest. I had to get us both out of there. The door…I found the door. Searching for the bolts, I slid them across. Now the latch, I winced at the hot metal.

Mary stopped wriggling and was quiet now. With desperation I half tumbled into the street trying to take long, hard gasps of air but the smoke poured out and still choked me, I couldn't breathe. With my eyes streaming, I clutched Mary tightly, afraid to let her go. Then I heard her cough and whimper as I collapsed and fell to the ground holding Mary to my chest.

'I can see something. Look, there's somebody there,' I heard a man shout.

People appeared from nowhere and were running towards me and Mary. I could hear the banging of doors and see lots of feet. Someone grabbed hold of my arm and dragged us away from the house then took Mary off me. I could feel the cold air and began to take in deep breaths. It felt good even though I could still feel the burning from inside. Voices were shouting for buckets of water and it all seemed to be happening in slow motion. Where was my Mam?

I half crawled to the other side of the road, and sat on the floor, cross legged and silent. It was dark but the fire lit up everything. I listened and stared towards the upstairs window expecting to see my Mam but the flames and sparks leapt up to the sky hiding everything from view. Someone wrapped something around my shoulders as the window glass exploded upstairs, shattering tiny pieces everywhere. I waited and listened for my Mam's voice but could hear no sound other than the fire and the voices of the people that were helping. I looked around for my family. Where were they? Sparks flew in all directions. Our neighbours were calling to each other and bringing buckets of water they filled from the community tap around the corner to throw onto the fire.

With a clatter and clip clop of hooves, the fire cart arrived, the horse snorting as it strained in the shafts. Now there were firemen joining the shouting and noise as I watched them working hard dampening the flames, and the buckets kept on coming. There was still no sign of my Mam, step-dad and my two younger brothers. I heard people talking and they seemed to be talking to me but from a distance away and I couldn't answer. Tears were streaming down my cheeks and then I could feel my body begin to shake.

I didn't notice who it was but one kindly neighbour cleaned, bathed and bandaged my hands and feet. They hurt, and before they were bandaged I could see the skin on my hands all curled up showing the raw flesh beneath. I watched the house and told myself that everyone must have escaped and they would be all right. When anyone attempted to move me I refused to go. I must wait for my Mam.

Seth, my step-father would have got away, I thought. He always looked after himself so he should be somewhere. I looked around but couldn't see him. Maybe he and my Mam were somewhere else with my brothers. They'll come to join me in a minute, I told myself. Then another thought struck me. Oh no! What if only Seth gets out? I really hoped that wouldn't happen because I knew I'd get some real beatings then.

I heard someone say, 'Poor soul…you're very brave saving your little sister.'

'What's going to happen to these children?' someone else shouted.

After what seemed ages, I felt my Auntie Lizzie put her arms around me and heard her sob as she hugged me tightly.

'You poor mite, what a horrible thing to happen…and look at your hands and feet.' Auntie Lizzie looked around 'Where's everyone else?' I shook my head. I only wish I knew. 'Ruth, where's the rest of them?' My Auntie's voice grew louder. 'I was told you were all right.' I sat quietly but saw someone nod to Auntie Lizzie and point to a door behind us. Auntie Lizzie got hold of my arm.

'Come on love, you can't sit there all night. We'll have to find the rest of them.'

I suppose she was right so I got up from the floor and still in a daze and limping badly, allowed Auntie Lizzie to help me to Mrs. Holt's door. Auntie Lizzie found it slightly ajar so she knocked and called.

'Mrs. Holt, are they all in here.'

'Come in.' Auntie Lizzie and I went in and found Mrs. Holt holding Mary who was now wrapped in a shawl. The old lady rocked to and fro in her rocking chair.

'A 'noo the'd come. It's a crying shame.' My Auntie Lizzie offered to take Mary off her but Mrs. Holt kept hold of her and began to sob. 'Poor souls.' The tears ran down her cheeks.

'Where are the rest of them?' Auntie Lizzie asked.

Mrs. Holt frowned. 'Thee dusna know does 'oo?' she said.

'What? Where's my Sister and the children?'

Mrs. Holt held Mary closer. 'They're gone lass…all gone.'

Auntie Lizzie gasped and fell backwards to sit on the nearest chair. 'They can't be…what do you mean gone?'

'They did'na ger out love.'

Auntie Lizzie screamed 'No-o-o.'

'Sit yersel' down lass, you've 'ad a nasty shock,' said Mrs. Holt who was being ever so kind.

'Oh my God, my Mam will go off her mind. Those poor, poor kids…and my Sister…'

Mrs. Holt nodded her head in sympathy, 'Gone love, all gone.'

'Oh, Mrs. Holt, at least someone saved the two children.'

'Ay, that's a blessing,' she said as she looked at me.

'Thanks a lot for sending for me. I really am grateful!' Auntie Lizzie cried.

'Well, y'ad to know. A towd 'em to fetch thee because a noo the'd come an' look a'ter 'em.'

'Thanks—it was thoughtful of you.'

'Y'ave Ruth to thank for savin' little 'un 'oo knows...she saved the babby.' Mrs.Holt passed Mary to Auntie Lizzie and hobbled over to the black leaded fireplace. Taking a small piece of frayed blanket that was airing on the oven door she passed it to Auntie Lizzie. 'Ere, tek this t' wrap the babby up in an' all. I dunna need it so I dunna wan' it back. It'll keep little un wa'm until thee gets wom 'cause it's still gor a nip in th'air. I found that piece of old towel for 'er nappy and I don't want that back either.' Auntie Lizzie gratefully accepted the blanket and swathed the baby in it. 'The'd better look a'ter Ruth, she's 'ad a bad shock.' Auntie Lizzie nodded, taking off the jacket that someone had placed around my shoulders, and she replaced it with her shawl, wrapping it around me.

'Can you give the jacket back to whomever it belongs to Mrs. Holt and thank them for me.'

'A will.Tak' care o' them two childer won't you?'

Auntie Lizzie nodded. 'I don't suppose they saved anything from the fire did they?'

'No love, there wasn't time.'

'I'll have to sort out some clothes for them tomorrow. If anyone enquires about the children tell them I've got them. They'll be safe with me and their Uncle Jim.'

Mrs. Holt nodded. Auntie Lizzie stepped out of the house with me and Mary. As we walked away another of the neighbours, a man, picked me up.

'Come on sunshine, I'll carry you,' he said, 'you can't walk like that.' I felt relieved as my feet were sore.

'Thank you, I'm grateful.' Auntie Lizzie looked at him and smiled. 'I couldn't carry them both.

'No bother,' he answered, 'I think this little lass has suffered enough.'

'Come on Ruth, let's go home.' Auntie Lizzie leaned over and kissed me lightly on my cheek. 'Grandma and Uncle Jim are waiting for us.'

'What about my Mam? She won't know where we are?' I looked up at her. 'I'm sure she must be wondering where me and Mary are. Can't we wait for her first? She'll be all right Aunty Lizzie, I'm sure.'

'I think you'd be better waiting for her at our house Ruth. C'mon love. I'm sure the neighbours will tell your Mam.'

She stopped abruptly and moved closer to the man who also hesitated. Auntie Lizzie attempted to wrap her shawl tighter around me to keep out the cold while holding the baby and whispered, 'You have me—and I love you very, very much. You also have your Uncle Jim and Grandma who are waiting for you now—and you still have your little sister.' Aunty Lizzie stroked my face. 'I'm so glad you escaped with the baby Ruth. You were very brave.' Aunty Lizzie carried Mary while the man carried me, we continued up the street as the morning light began to break. It had been a heck of a night, but now it was over and a new day was beginning. Maybe tomorrow things would be a little different when my Mam came for me with the boys.

§§§§§§

When we turned the corner of the street to go to Aunty Lizzie's we could see two people waiting for us. Uncle Jim looked very serious and as we got closer I watched as my Grandma tried not to cry but then she broke down and sobbed as she spoke.

'Where 'er rest of 'em?'

'Oh mam,' Aunty Lizzie said, 'there's only the two of them left.'

'No-o-oo.' My Grandma crumpled and dropped to the floor and Auntie Lizzie burst into tears.

Uncle Jim picked up my Grandma and carried her into the house, where he carefully placed her on the couch.

The man carried me into the house too and sat me down on a chair then he left. I stared at the fire that roared in the grate, then moved away to sit on the floor in the corner of the room at the back because it frightened me. I sat huddled watching Aunty Lizzie with Mary and I couldn't understand where my Mam was. Why wasn't she looking after Mary? Where were they all? They must be somewhere!

Uncle Jim was trying to bring my Grandma round by patting her face and whispering her name. He brought a damp cloth which he placed on her forehead.

'Mam, Mam.' Uncle Jim whispered and Grandma opened her eyes and sat up slowly. Her eyes were heavy and for a short time she didn't move, then she shivered when she looked at me and found her voice.

'Tha knows, that shiver ran down mi spine and through mi body when a thowt o' what must 'ave 'appened. Whar 'appened to my daughter…and the boys?'

I didn't know so I couldn't tell her so I sat quietly watching and listening. Where was Seth? I only hoped he wasn't stopping them from joining me at Auntie Lizzie's, only I knew what he was like.

Uncle Jim poked at the fire then stoked it up again before hurrying upstairs. He returned with a drawer.

'I've taken this from the chest in the bedroom and put the things from there in the other drawers in case you want to know Lizzie.'

I watched him prepare the drawer for Mary. 'Where's my mam and the lads?' I asked.

Uncle Jim and Auntie Lizzie looked at each other.

'Don't worry about that now dear.' Aunty Lizzie looked busy, 'We'll sort all that out tomorrow when you've had a good night's rest.'

'But where are they now?' I asked again.

'I'll prepare a bath for you and then you can get that smoke out of your hair.' Uncle Jim said as he bustled about.

Uncle Jim disappeared into the back yard and returned carrying the tin bath. Soon he had it filled and ready for me.

'Can you get me a bowl Jim then I can wash her hair?' Auntie Lizzie called then she put her hand on my arm.

'Come on love but keep your feet and hands out of the water. Look, I'll put this towel over the end of the bath to make it more comfortable for your feet.'

Uncle Jim came and placed the bowl down by our side and returned to the kitchen. Auntie Lizzie helped me to take off the dress which was now dirty then picked me up and carefully placed me in the bath. I put my feet on the towel at the end.

'We'll wash that smoke out of your hair' she fussed. 'I'm sure you'll feel better when you get cleaned up. 'Poor Ruth! You have had a bad time.' I felt as if I was going to cry. Everyone was so kind, even Uncle Jim. Seth was never like that with me.

The bath felt good. It was warm and soothing. Aunty Lizzie was ever so careful as she washed me and helped me from the bath. Gently patting me dry she wrapped the towel around my shoulders and half carried me to a chair.

'Just sit there a minute, I won't be long. I'll just run upstairs and find you something to wear in bed love.'

Auntie Lizzie ran upstairs and returned with an old dress of hers. She combed my hair, and I caught her with a handful of it as she was trying to hide it.

'Is that my hair Auntie Lizzie?'

'It is.' I'm afraid it's burned, singed, but I'll trim your hair tomorrow then it won't show. What do you think, Ruth?' I nodded. 'After a good night's sleep you'll feel a lot better love.'

Grandma Tyson stood up and asked, 'Would you like a nice cup of coc'a afore you go t' bed love?' I felt too tired to talk anymore so nodded my head. 'Come on Lizzie I'll help you sort 'em out.' Aunty Lizzie refused to let her but she wouldn't listen. 'Let me help Lizzie, I don't want to sit and think about things.'

'You can help by looking after Mary for a few minutes,' Aunty Lizzie answered.

Uncle Jim made the cocoa, and toasted some crumpets on the fire then spread them with butter. They tasted good and I really enjoyed them. It had been a long time since I ate anything so I felt very hungry.

Grandma sat and watched me. 'I bet the'll be ready for that, in fact, I bet thi could eat a bull an' a biscuit eh Ruth?' I nodded. 'If you geritt all ett'n, p'raps

Uncle Jim'll mak' you more…if you're still 'ungry,' urged Grandma, 'it'll d' thee gud.'

I didn't like to appear greedy so I nodded my head but didn't speak. The crumpets did taste good but maybe it was enough to eat before I went to bed. I remembered my Mam's words. 'You mustn't eat much before you go to bed as it lies on your stomach and that doesn't do you any good,' and I was having trouble swallowing anyway, my throat was so sore.

Grandma took Mary into the kitchen where she bathed her and soon she was ready for bed.

'Go and light the gas mantles, Jim,' asked Aunty Lizzie.

Uncle Jim went upstairs and lit the gas mantles in both the bedrooms we were using while Auntie Lizzie tucked Mary into the drawer that Uncle Jim placed by their bed. Auntie Lizzie asked me to say my prayers before I climbed into bed. I didn't believe in God as he'd never listened to me when I asked him for anything before, and now this. I didn't argue though. I kneeled at the side of the bed, closed my eyes and placed my hands together like my Mam told me to do. 'Dear God, please find my Mam and the lads. I love them very much and I'm worrying about them. Can you send them here then I know they're all right?' I thought that's enough so climbed into bed and Auntie Lizzie placed a kiss on my forehead then tucked me in.

'Goodnight my love. I hope you sleep. Don't worry; me and my Mam and Uncle Jim will look after you and Mary.' As she left the bedroom she called, 'I'll leave the gas light on and the door open just in case you need me, although your Grandma will be coming up to bed soon.' I noticed my Auntie Lizzie had tears in her eyes that she wiped away as she left me to go downstairs.

I watched the shadows made by the gas light as it hissed and popped and could hear the three grown ups washing the pots and discussing the last few hours. Uncle Jim talked about my family dying in the fire. No, that couldn't be right. They can't be dead. We just didn't know where they were, they'd see.

I snuggled lower into the bed. It was comfortable and warm and smelled of Grandma. Later, I heard Grandma's soft footsteps on the stairs. Keeping my eyes shut I listened to the sound of her undressing. Grandma turned the gas mantle off before she climbed into bed with me. My Auntie and Uncle came upstairs and I could hear the bedsprings squeak with their weight as they climbed into bed in the next room. Soon I heard my Grandma sobbing. I lay a while and re-lived the past few hours again in my mind as far as I could remember. Surely my Mam and brothers weren't dead. They couldn't be. I was only playing with them a few hours ago. Just before I fell asleep, I wiped the tears away that were tickling my nose.

Chapter 2

It was summer, three years later and Auntie Lizzie told me she had booked for me to go on a Sunday school trip in a wagonette to the seaside but Mary couldn't go as it was too far for her. As I had never been away from home before and never even seen the sea I became really excited. When the day arrived the sun shone with the promise of a lovely day and Auntie Lizzie gave me a severe warning.

'You have to acclimatise first before you go in the sea and you won't have time for that so don't be tempted to paddle or you'll get a chill.'

We travelled for a long time and I thoroughly enjoyed the views and seeing places I had never seen before. There were fields of cows and sheep, plus horses. People waved to us as we drove past and we waved back in return until eventually we saw Blackpool Tower. It was very tall and seemed to move from the right side of the road to the left and then back again. Some of the children thought that someone was moving it but I guessed it was the way the roads twisted and turned that made it look that way.

I became very excited. I couldn't wait to see the sea and the sand. I'd heard tales about them but now I was going to see them and I hoped I wouldn't be disappointed. There were lots of seagulls flying around and screeching and it was an experience I will never forget. The air smelled different, it was fresher and…different. I took a deep breath and it made me feel good. We parked not very far from the sea and I couldn't wait to get on the sands. I was amazed when I walked onto the beach at the amount of sand there, and the sea I thought was amazing too. Some of the other girls immediately took off their shoes and ran into the water. There were people sitting in chairs, some lying on the sands and going to sleep and quite a lot of people in the sea, either paddling or swimming. Some of the children were playing ball and some were digging in the sand. It seemed such fun. I looked out to sea; it appeared to go on forever and ever as you couldn't see the end of it.

'C'mon Ruth, take off your shoes and join us,' some of the others called.

'I daren't. Auntie Lizzie told me I mustn't.'

'Auntie Lizzie's not here, she won't know. C'mon, it's lovely.' One of them shouted as she ran into the water again until it was up to her knees. I envied her.

Watching the waves rolling onto the sand I did feel tempted. The others were laughing and having fun so I couldn't resist any more and took off my shoes and stockings and ran to the sea for a paddle. The others called words of encouragement as I ran over the sands towards them and eventually I reached the sea and allowed the water to trickle over my feet. It was surprisingly cold and I kept jumping in and out of the water squealing before I could stand for a while and allow the waves to lap over my toes. After a while I waded further into the water being careful not to get too wet as I did feel pangs of guilt because of what my Auntie Lizzie said. We played for a long time digging in the sand with our hands and watching the sea fill the holes we made plus other games we invented. One of the boys found a crab and threw it at one of the girls, she screamed and ran but the boys thought it was funny. I hoped they didn't throw one at me as I think I would have screamed too. There were shells to be gathered and I saved a few to take home for Mary. I watched families playing games together and fathers making sand castles for their children. As I didn't have a spade it was difficult but I had a go anyway. It didn't compare to the others but I felt proud of my castle until one of the other girls accidentally trod on it. After we dried ourselves we all clambered onto the toastrack tram that took us on a circular tour of Blackpool. I thoroughly enjoyed that.

It was an exciting day and home seemed a long way off as the wagonette bumped and trundled along the road. I could feel my head nodding. I was sleepy. When I eventually arrived home I told all the family about my day and how the other children paddled in the water, especially Mary, as I showed her the shells I collected.

'Smell them Mary. You can smell the sea.' I didn't tell them that I'd picked them up from the water while I was paddling. The following morning I couldn't even remember going to bed the previous night.

A few weeks later and I skipped down the street on my way home from playing with a friend after school. There were children having a game of hop scotch on the street and I love playing that but it was close to tea time and my tummy rumbled in anticipation. As I reached closer to home there were loud voices coming from a side street and turning the corner I found Uncle George arguing with a woman.

Uncle George wasn't really my proper uncle because he was the brother of my late step-father Seth. There were a few in the family but Uncle George was the only one that Seth spoke to. Very often when I saw him he had at least one woman on his arm. I suppose he was good looking but he did smell a bit because he didn't look after himself enough and he wasn't a nice man. I remember the times he called on the family when I lived at home. If we tried to play with him he'd get angry and tell us to go away and leave him alone and not in a very nice way. Uncle Jim didn't mind us playing games with him, well, tormenting him really, when he called with Auntie Lizzie but Seth didn't make them very welcome. Seth and Uncle George lived together after their parents died but now Uncle George lived alone, except when there was a woman living with him. The women came and went and no one knew who would open the door when you knocked, or so I'd overheard someone say. My mam did mention once that the other members of Seth's family didn't get on with the two brothers but I didn't know why for sure. I do remember Uncle George calling at the house when Seth wasn't in. As I didn't like him, I went upstairs to make the beds. While I was busy I heard a slap and my Mam's voice.

'Don't you do that again or I'll tell Seth,' I heard my Mam say, 'Now go home.' When I asked my Mam what he had done, she wouldn't tell me.

Now Uncle George was shouting at the woman, and then hit her across the face. A man across the street shouted, 'Oy, stop that.'

'Mind your own bloody business,' Uncle George shouted back. 'It's nothing to do with you.'

Uncle George then grabbed the woman's shoulders and began to shake her. I stopped and wondered if I should say something but decided against it and began to run away as fast as I could. I remembered how Seth would lose his temper when I lived at home and I would get the brunt of it. This time I didn't intend to give Uncle George a chance to pick on me.

Once Mary and I went living with our Aunty, Uncle and Grandma, I hardly ever saw Uncle George, unless it was on this kind of occasion where he was making a nuisance of himself. He wasn't nice but neither was my stepfather, Seth, who could be cruel with my Mam and my brothers and I.

Only Mary was his, as our real dad died in a pit accident when little Jimmy, my youngest brother were three. I had another brother, John, and he was less than a year younger than me, but they were both gone, perished in the fire, and I did miss them. I missed my Mam a lot too. When my Mam married Seth, it was not a good day. No one could understand why she married him, especially Auntie Lizzie and Grandma but most of all me. I would hear people whispering behind their backs whenever my Mam and Seth were out together, which weren't very often, and then after Mary was born, no one asked any more questions.

Seth often beat us, and with anything that was handy but mostly the belt from off his trousers. Woe betide one of us if we ran off while he was struggling to untie his belt, because then he'd hit us even more when we did return home. We were terrified of him. He sometimes picked up a chair and threw that at us too. He'd even threatened John with his open razor once and that really started an argument with my Mam. Almost everything was broken, ornaments, furniture, nothing escaped, and he'd even broken my Mam's wrist once. Poor mam got the worst of it. She would often wear a few bruises, especially if she tried to stop him from taking the money out of her purse for beer. I didn't have any of that anymore. Now I knew only love and kindness.

Grandma Tyson came out of the house as I arrived home. 'I'm just on mi' way t' see Ethel. Behave yoursel' and look a'ter Mary.'

Grandma's friend Ethel had a greengrocers shop and Grandma helped her a few hours a week. There were fruit and vegetables to go through to sort out the good from the bad. Grandma would bring some of it home if it was too bad to sell but not too bad to use and that helped to feed us all. Soft fruits that were over ripe were made into jam and pies and I welcomed them because they tasted so good with Grandma's pastry.

I watched my Grandma walk down the street until she turned the corner, I do love her, and then I went inside the house. The smell of freshly baked bread still lingered in the kitchen and she had left two loaves and six muffins on the table to cool off. The sight of them made me feel even hungrier. I hesitated, should I take a muffin? I could imagine it well buttered and smothered with her home made jam. My fingers lingered for a while but I thought better of it. I didn't want to get into trouble. Everything seemed quiet so I went to look for Auntie Lizzie and found her busy in the sewing room. Auntie Lizzie mended, re-styled and made clothes for people to help the money spin out, and her clients were mixed from the rich, the councillor's wives, to the poor. Her reputation was good and she was popular. Not wanting to disturb my Auntie by asking for something to eat, I decided instead to go out again.

'Is it okay if I call on my friend Doris Auntie Lizzie?'

'Of course dear, but don't be late for your tea. I did hope that you would watch Mary but if you tell her she must play in the big back, close to the yard gate, then she should be all right.'

I gave in to my hunger pains. 'Can I have a biscuit only I'm a bit hungry,' I asked.

'Okay, but only have one as we will be eating soon and I don't want you to spoil your tea.'

As I went into the middle room I could smell polish. My Grandma had been busy. As I searched the cupboards for a biscuit I remembered to only use the handles to avoid my fingerprints all over the furniture as I'd been told. Eventually I found the tin where she kept them.

I ate the biscuit on the way to see Doris and stayed there a while. We talked about our day at school and then I realised I hadn't checked on Mary. I quickly left and went home. Going outside to the yard I opened the door to the big back but I couldn't see her. It was too quiet and that was unusual when she was around so I searched the house but there was still no sign of her. I went looking for my Auntie

'Where's Mary?' Aunty Lizzie was still sewing.

'Isn't she in the big back?'

'I've looked but I can't see her.'

'Did you tell her to stay in the back?'

'I meant to but I forgot. I'm sorry!'

Auntie Lizzie put her sewing down and shook her head. 'She knows she shouldn't go out of the back but she has a mind of her own that one.'

We both went out to the big back and looked around, then to the front of the house but there was no sign of Mary. Panic set in.

'Go and see if she's with any of her friends and I'll go and ask the neighbours if they've seen her,' Aunty Lizzie said as she left the house. It was tea time and after the hot day the air was heavy with black clouds beginning to form. 'We'll have to find her quickly Ruth,' Auntie called, 'I think it's going to rain.'

As we were searching, Uncle Jim came home and joined us. Grandma returned from seeing her friend Ethel so she stayed in the house while we carried on our search. I walked the streets, calling Mary's name. I asked her friends but nobody had seen her for a while. Auntie Lizzie went looking on the canal, which was close to our home, but she said there was no sign of Mary. Calling on the neighbours, I asked if they had seen any sign of Mary but none had. Meanwhile, Grandma Tyson kept watch from the doorstep.

As I walked by Uncle George's house, he stepped out in front of me so I asked him. 'Have you seen Mary Uncle George?' Although I often avoided him, this time I couldn't.

'No!' He looked me up and down and stepped closer. I could smell the stale beer on his breath. 'You're growing up to be a little smasher, just like your mam, aren't you?' He lifted his hand as if to touch me but I slipped out of his way. I don't trust him and I haven't the time.

'Why don't you come and live with me Ruth? We could have a bit of fun.'

I was a little unsure of what he meant by fun, but I knew in my own mind that it wasn't playing games like Snake and Ladders, so I ran up the street, looking back to make sure Uncle George wasn't following me. There were a few children using a rope on a lamp post as a swing, so I stopped and asked if they'd seen Mary but they all shook their heads. I saw other children playing and asked them too but none of them had seen Mary and I worried. As I neared home I heard voices. I looked over the boundary fence that guarded the embankment where it sloped down to the river. There were lads playing games around and under the bridge across the road from the house and I heard them challenging each other to dive off the bridge. At this point the river made a pool, and the water would be warm because the mills along the valley emptied their surplus water from the boilers into it in the early evening so it was a popular place to swim. All the young people who lived nearby knew there was a gap in the fence where they could climb through and on days like this they often did. Some of them brought a picnic which mostly consisted of a jam sandwich and a bottle of water.

Squeezing myself through the gap I reached the grassy embankment and looked down towards the rushing water. There were rocks hidden by the weeds that grew in abundance and it made me think that Mary couldn't possibly be down there, but then I saw her. She stood on a rock close to another deep pool where the current was strong. Obviously the boys were too intent with their games to notice her and I could feel a cold shiver run down my spine at the thought of what she would do. I opened my mouth to call her but I was too late. Mary stepped into the water, disappearing quickly beneath it.

I screamed as I ran down the slope, almost falling on my way to the river and shouted hysterically to the boys, 'Get her—get her…she'll drown.' The boys must have heard me as they stopped their fooling around and looked my way.

'She's gone under…there…no there, I pointed to the place where I last saw Mary, and one of them swam towards where I pointed. He dived under the water, disappearing for a while before he surfaced again and took another deep breath. Going under the water he again returned to the surface where the other boys joined him. Instantly, one of them saw Mary's arm in the fast moving water, and the first boy dived again in the direction they pointed. He was missing possibly for a few seconds but it seemed a long time before he reappeared with a seemingly unconscious Mary. Between them the boys brought Mary to the side of the river, and I dragged my sister onto the grass. I lay her on her side and smacked her on her back. I once heard that you had to do that. The boy threw himself on the grass. He looked exhausted but grinned when he heard Mary start coughing.

'She's opened her eyes,' I said with relief. Eventually, Mary began to cry. All the boys were congratulating the one who saved her and I heard them call him Billy. After assuring myself Mary was recovering I turned to him.

'Thanks, she's my little sister and I should have been there to stop her.' I felt overcome and leaned over to kiss him on his cheek. I got wet as his hair was dripping down his face, so I wiped my face with the back of my hand as the others all cheered. Billy blushed pink.

'No worry.' He looked embarrassed.

'Why you hit me Wuth?' Mary cried. 'You hurt.'

'I had to.'

One of Billy's friends came over with something wrapped in cloth and tied with string.

'Do you want to open this thing that you found Billy?'

'I'd forgotten that.' Turning to me he explained. 'I found it half buried in the mud when I dived off the bridge. It was on the bottom of the river over there, among a load of rubbish.'

'More than likely dead kittens or something horrid.' I pulled my face.

'You never know, it could be treasure although it did feel a bit lumpy.'

Billy tried to undo the string but couldn't. 'Have one of you got a knife?' he asked. One of them went and found his trousers and brought back a penknife. Billy cut the string. They all crowded round to see what was in the parcel. As he took away the cloth, he yelled 'It's a knife,' and placed the open parcel on to the ground.

'It is a knife,' one of the other lads said, among other things.'

I looked down at the parcel and I could see the long blade with a beautifully patterned handle and there were other things too. One of the boys picked up a cloth that was rolled up inside and shook it out.

'It's a shirt,' one of them said.

'And it's ripped,' I added.

Another cloth turned out to be a scarf. Under those were a bracelet, earrings, gold locket and chain and a carriage clock.

I looked at the gold locket and chain and held it up. 'I've always wanted one of these, but I think this one's been stolen.' I thought no one would throw things like that away, so it had to be stolen, and there was me, longing for a gold locket. They looked ever so posh.

'Look inside, it could have a picture in it,' one of the boys said.

I gave it to Billy. 'You open it.'

Billy opened it. 'It's a woman but I don't know who she is. It's a little worse for wear anyway, you can't tell, I think the waters got to it.'

I looked at it followed by the others but none of us recognised the woman in the photograph.

The boys all looked at each other a little dubiously and then Billy wrapped them all up again. I stood up and helped Mary to her feet. 'You'd better take them to the police and tell them where you found them.'

'I would Billy,' one of the boys agreed.

'I'm taking Mary home before she gets her death.' I held Mary's hand. 'Come on you little madam, I don't know what your Auntie's going to say.'

'Do you think I'll be in twouble Ruthie?'

'We'll have to wait and see, but don't ever do it again.'

'Don't forget her shoes?' one of the boys called.

When I looked round he was holding Mary's shoes up so I took them off him.

'Thanks!' I turned to Mary. 'You took your shoes off before you went in the river. That's a good girl but you must never do anything like that again…you could have died Mary,' and I shivered at the thought.

'I wanted to paddle…like Bwackpool, like you told me,' Mary said sniffling as she spoke. 'I was hot.'

'You must never try paddling when you're on your own. You don't know how deep it is, and that's why you almost drowned.'

I helped Mary on with her shoes then helped my little sister up the banking as she was exhausted. I thought I'd better be careful in future of what I tell her. When I arrived home I told the family about Mary and the find in the river and the grown ups just looked at each other but didn't say a word about it. Meanwhile, Mary received a good scolding from Grandma Tyson and after a bath, was sent to bed with nothing to eat or drink.

When I went to bed later, I could hear the grown ups talking about a murder that had taken place a few months before. As the newspapers were always hidden from me, I didn't know anything about it. Could those things found in the river have something to do with that murder? It seemed very suspicious.

Chapter 3

The following year on a late Saturday afternoon, Auntie Lizzie & Uncle Jim took us to Ashton market for some shopping. Uncle Jim would be at work most Saturdays, so they took advantage of the day.

There were some lovely smells and Mary and I couldn't wait to see what the market had to offer. It was a fairyland to us and we watched with interest when one of the stallholders boiled sugar and Uncle Jim told us to watch what the man did when it was ready, but Auntie Lizzie didn't like it.

'That smell makes me feel quite sick.'

'Look at the children Lizzie, I don't think they agree with you,' Uncle Jim laughed so they stopped there for a while.

I was excited, and so was Mary. When it was ready, we watched as the man poured it onto a metal table and added the essence and Mary shouted with delight when he began to make the sweets. It was magic! Auntie Lizzie and Uncle Jim allowed us to have two pennyworths but we had to choose between all the delicious varieties and that wasn't easy. Mary was only allowed small ones but choosing one was difficult.

Next, it was a treat for Auntie Lizzie and Uncle Jim at the black pudding stall. Here they boiled them, split them and placed them on a muffin. Auntie and Uncle chose to have a bit of mustard on theirs and I pulled my face at them as they paid the man their two pence each. As we walked away, I watched the mustard running down Uncle Jim's fingers and shivered, but Uncle Jim licked it off.

'That's the best part Ruthie. I know licking your fingers isn't allowed at home but out here it's different.'

'Really Jim, you shouldn't set that kind of example to the children.' Auntie Lizzie said with disgust.

After the shopping, we called on Uncle Jim's brother Ted, who lived in Ashton. Uncle Ted and Auntie Susannah had a six year old son called Peter who was two years older than Mary. I cuddled him and Mary cried with jealousy. The adults watched me with the children. Auntie Susannah asked Lizzie if I would be allowed to call every Saturday morning and help her with Peter, plus do a few odd chores and they would pay me.

'What do you think Ruth?' asked Auntie Lizzie.

I nodded my head. It was arranged that I would start next Saturday. Uncle Ted would meet me on the main road and take me to the house, because Uncle Jim was working, and when I was sure I could find my own way then I would go on my own.

When we left them, I thought about my little job. I would have a bit of money to call my own. I could buy Mary little things that she liked and maybe treat myself to some sweets sometime. My thoughts were very busy so by the time we reached home I was too sleepy for my supper and went to bed, falling asleep as soon as my head touched the pillow.

Uncle Ted came to collect me the following Saturday morning to take me to Auntie Susannah's before he started work. My duties were explained to me, I was expected to sweep the street at the front of the house, Donkey stone the window-sill and door step, then go and clean inside the house. Windows needed cleaning before lunch sometime but after I was expected to take over looking after Peter to give his mother a break. I worked hard in the morning and took Peter out in the afternoon if the weather was dry. It gave me something to look forward to and Peter enjoyed it too. If the weather was sunny and warm then I would ask Auntie Susannah if we could take a small picnic with us, a slice of jam and bread each and a bottle of water was packed in a bag and it always seemed to taste better when it was a picnic. We would visit the park where I would allow Peter to play on the swings and then play mother and sit and watch him.

Grandma Tyson was spending a lot more time with her friend Ethel. She worked in the shop but came home to do some housework and make meals when necessary. She told us that Ethel was feeling lonely after she lost her husband, so she felt obliged to spend time with her.

A few weeks later Uncle Jim's youngest sister Beth, got married and came to live with us with her new husband Percy, so I helped my Auntie to clear out the spare bedroom for them. They had to ask around for beds as there wasn't a spare. Uncle Ted and Aunty Susannah had a single bed they weren't using, and one of the neighbours said they could use the bed that belonged to their son who had been killed in a pit accident. We didn't tell Beth and Percy the story of that bed. They picked up orange boxes from somewhere, cleaned and smoothed them to use instead of drawers for their clothes.

Auntie Lizzie said, 'I don't think I'm the most popular woman giving them single beds but at least they have somewhere to sleep.'

Percy worked at the pit and came home looking dirty so he would have a bath in front of the fire in the sewing room. Auntie Lizzie wasn't allowed in there while he bathed and Ruth could see that although she didn't say much she would get annoyed as it stopped her from doing her sewing. For a while the house always seemed full of people and getting ready in the morning was taken in turns at the sink in the kitchen.

Beth kept Ruth laughing as she would tell her tales from her days in service.

'I'd iron the master's shoelaces.'

I looked at her in awe. 'What for?'

'They had to be done. The master liked them freshly pressed in the morning and the newspaper too if it was creased. Then I would polish the silver with leathers and rouge.'

'I've never seen silver, except for teaspoons.'

Laughing, Beth answered 'No, and you'll more than likely never will my dear unless of course you become a servant like me.'

I pulled my face. 'I don't think I will.'

Beth laughed. 'I would brush the mistresses hair too after I helped her undress and put on her nightgown.'

'Did you ever pull her hair when it tangled? Did she shout at you? or didn't it tangle like mine does?'

'So many questions young lady. I must admit that if she started on her 'better than you' attitude, I would sometimes pretend it had tangled and pull it a bit just to get my own back.' We both giggled.

'My duties were to rise early, light the fire, sweep and clean the kitchen and pantry then go and clean the stone steps at the front of the house…and that was in the morning.' Beth laughed and she had such a lovely laugh it sounded like an angel, not that I'd ever heard an angel laugh but I bet it sounded like Beth's.

'Didn't you get tired?' I asked.

'I'm getting tired talking about it. Let's change the subject.' We both giggled again.

Beth sometimes took me shopping and bought me a little something like a small reading book or writing pad. When Percy came home, he would have a bath then they would sit together and Percy would put his arm round Beth's shoulders. If they thought no one was looking they'd kiss. They looked very happy and I hoped I would find someone like Percy one day. When they left six months later to rent their own house, I really missed them, especially Beth as she was always laughing. First thing in the morning I would awaken to her laughter. Of course, it could have been her laughter that awoke me in the first place but I didn't care, I just loved to hear Beth laugh. The only good thing to come out of it when they left, was that my Auntie told me and Mary that we could have our own bedroom as Grandma was sleeping at Ethel's now. From sharing with Grandma and now our own bedroom, life was looking up. Auntie did say though that Grandma's bed would stay in Mary's room so that if she changed her mind she could still sleep there.

Chapter 4

I finished working for Auntie Susannah when I left school and took a job in the mill with Doris, my friend, who lived a few doors away.

Although it was exciting, it was frightening too. I had never seen such an amount of machinery before and it was so noisy. I wondered how people could hold a conversation with each other with all that going on. When I went to bed the night before I started at the mill there were my usual nightmares of the fire. Every time I had some kind of stress, I would dream of it. It was always about my life as a child, my beatings off Seth and shortage of food, but always ended up with the fire.

As long as I lived I would never forget my first day at work. Usually, I didn't get up until there was a fire burning in the grate, but this morning I couldn't wait for my Uncle Jim to light it. After being up at five thirty with my Uncle I watched him lay the fire and use the bellows. It still didn't burn so he placed the shovel in front of the fire and wrapped the evening paper round it from the night before.

'That should draw it. It'll soon be blazing,' Uncle Jim said with satisfaction. Poor Uncle Jim must do that every morning before he goes to work, I thought, and felt grateful for the warmth he provided. When he left for work I waited for Doris to knock for me. As soon as I heard the knock I could feel the butterflies in my stomach. I opened the door and stood on the doorstep.

'Are you ready?' Doris asked.

I took my shawl from the nail on the wall and wrapped it around me before slipping into my clogs. 'I've never been up this early before, isn't it dark?' Doris nodded her head. 'Oh Doris, I'm terrified aren't you? Did you sleep?'

'Not flipping likely. I just hope we can do it.' Doris trembled and I felt sorry for her, after all, didn't I know what she was going through?

'Don't be silly,' I answered, 'I'm sure we can. They'll teach us.' Doris seemed even worse than I did. Linking her arm I squeezed it, 'You'll be fine.'

Walking out at this time in the morning was strange. We knew the river well but not at this time of day. It was dark and chilly and the trees rustling in the wind seemed eerie. There was no sound of birds, just the gushing of the water as it fell over the stones and rushed on its way. There were other people walking in the same direction as us, their clogs making a familiar echoing noise on the cobbled streets. Lamp lights gave a strange glow too.

'Hiya! Are you on the way to the mill?' A boy caught us up and began to walk with us.

'Yes,' I said, 'it's our first day. Do you work in the mill?'

'I do and have done for two years now.'

'Is it all right,' Doris found her voice.

'It's fine, and of course you get paid for it. Not like school.'

They reached a street lamp and Ruth caught sight of his face. 'Is your name Billy?'

'Yes, I remember you too. Do you remember the last time we met?'

'Yes, I do.' My mind returned to the day when Mary disappeared and I found her by the river. 'You were my hero that day.'

'I remember the kiss I got for that.'

I could feel my cheeks getting hot. 'Do you?'

'You didn't tell me that Ruth,' Doris said giving me a nudge.

'Did you ever find out about the parcel you found in the mud at the bottom of the river,' I asked.

'No, but I think, and I don't care what they say, that it was the knife that was used in the murder of that toff from that big house. The more I thought about it the more sure I am.'

'I thought so too at the time, but there's never been anything in the papers about it or I'm sure I would have known.'

'Have you ever thought…you could know the murderer?'

'What makes you say that?' Ruth asked.

'Well, you never know do you? It could be anybody.'

'I don't think I know anyone who could commit murder,' I said with a shiver running down my spine.

'I know it's not nice to think you could know a murderer. I mean…you just don't know.'

'That isn't a very nice thought…knowing a murderer,' I could feel Doris shudder as she spoke. We walked without speaking for a while and I was deep in thought.

'Are you working at the mill on the valley?' Billy asked.

'Yes! Why? do you work there?'

'I most certainly do.' He smiled down at me.

'That's nice.' My fears began to disappear.

When we walked into the factory, it was like another world. The smell, the noise and the machines, it was different. Large machines I had never seen before like spinning and weaving machines which were so noisy. The rooms were big with high ceilings and fluff floating everywhere that made it look as if it was snowing. At first I couldn't hold a conversation but very soon learned to read lips.

My mind wandered back to Billy, his friendly face and cheeky smile. It must be fate that we were working at the same mill. Later as Doris and I were working at our machines I watched Billy with my heart in my mouth. He did the most dangerous things like walking between machines that came far too close for comfort. It was his job but I thought it was far too dangerous for anyone to work under those conditions. Billy moved quickly, and I both admired him and looked forward to getting to know him better. Every morning after that, he would catch up with us as we walked to work.

Both Doris and I were learning to use a knotter to tie the cotton, we both found it difficult. How did the others do it? They didn't seem to have a problem with theirs. It wasn't long before mine broke so after struggling with it for a while; I took it to the charge hand.

'I'm sorry but it's broken. Can you mend it for me please?' I asked and I could feel myself blushing, I felt such a fool.

'Call yourself a winder? Huh, I don't know what the world's coming to.'

I thought; I'm a winder. Is that what I am? After returning to Doris I said, 'Do you know we're called winders?'

'Yes, he told us that when we started.'

'I mustn't have heard him.'

Excitement, I guess,' Doris replied.

After that I learned to use the knotter and felt ever so proud. I mastered the knotter before Doris and was given a few ends of my own to look after.

When I arrived home that evening full of news of my day, I put it aside when I heard raised voices before I even opened the front door. This was unusual, but it was Auntie Lizzie and she wasn't pleased with Mary.

'Whatever's the matter?' I asked.

'Ask your sister,' Auntie Lizzie looked very upset.

Mary had tears in her eyes. 'I'm sorry Auntie, I didn't mean to spoil it 'cause it was a lovely hat and I liked it.'

'What's she done?' I asked.

'What's she done?' Lizzie repeated. She only took a customer's hat while the poor woman was trying on a dress. It disappeared and we couldn't find it anywhere.'

As Lizzie depended on the money she made making and mending clothes, I knew her reputation was important.

Mary began to cry. 'I'm sorry, I didn't mean it.'

'Oh Mary!' I frowned.

Lizzie looked at me and winked. 'And it was Mrs. Hutton's too.'

I remembered that woman as someone poor Auntie Lizzie couldn't please so how hard she tried. Things were never quite right for her. If it wasn't the right buttons then the beads were wrong. She just picked at everything. 'Not Mrs. Hutton?' I pulled my face at Auntie Lizzie. 'What did she do to it?'

'When we found it…with Mary, in the big back where she was playing, she had worn it and dropped it on the floor…it had been raining too. Can you imagine it Ruth?'

I tried hard not to laugh and attempted to put on a stern face, 'I can. Oh Mary what are we going to do with you?'

'When Mrs. Hutton arrived here, the hat had some lovely flowers and ribbon on it but they didn't look so lovely when we found it full of mud, and now Mary's going to bed for being a naughty girl. Go on with you.' Mary cried and ran off and up the stairs.

'You should have seen it Ruth. I wanted to laugh but I knew I daren't. Mrs. Hutton would never see the funny side of it. It took me all my time to keep a straight face. I don't know, but it couldn't have happened to a grumpier customer. It looked as if the child kicked it around for a while and the ribbon looked dirty and wet.'

'I think with Mary's enthusiasm for hats she's going to make a good milliner,' I giggled.

'Such a fuss, i' wo'alreet, jus' mucky,' Grandma added.

'All the same mam, we can't allow her to do that kind of thing.'

When I went to bed that night I lay thinking of how my life was changing. From school to work with a wage packet to look forward to, I was now in the adult world and being treated as such, plus, I've met Billy again and life was getting interesting.

The next Monday morning, Doris and I went to work and the charge hand brought a new girl in. To our surprise it was Alice, an old friend who had suffered with diphtheria when we were at school. I hadn't seen her for ages. I knew she'd been in hospital and I'd seen her being pushed around in a pram because she couldn't walk but now she looked fine.

'I didn't know you were starting here,' I smiled at her, 'how are you?'

'My Mam said she wanted me to learn to type and work in an office as she thought I wouldn't be strong enough for this but I insisted on coming here and joining you two.'

'Aww, that's nice.' Doris was enthusiastic. 'We can all come to work together.'

'Yes, and walk home together,' I added. Then I thought that maybe I could walk home with Billy without feeling guilty at abandoning Doris, that's if he liked me enough.

We all shared our lunch and discussed the latest songs but mainly boys, especially those that worked in the mill.

'Keep your eyes off Billy though,' I laughed, because I have *my* eyes on him.

'My eyes were looking his way I must admit.' She saw the startled look on my face and added, 'Don't worry, they're back now.' We both laughed. 'I was so much looking forward to working with you two as you were always laughing when you were together, and I always wondered what you laughed about.' Alice remarked.

'And now you know…we laugh at anything and nothing in particular,' I added. We all giggled until the charge-hand came over to see what the frivolity was all about.

'C'mon girls, get on with your work,' he said unsmiling.

Nights were getting darker and the frost and ice were on the inside of the windows of the house in the morning. I found it more difficult to get out of bed and snuggled into Mary who sometimes climbed into my bed when she felt cold. And it was mornings like this I felt glad of it.

'Come on sleepy head,' Uncle Jim called a few minutes later. 'It's foggy outside and it could take you a bit longer to get to work.'

Climbing out of bed, I yawned as I took the stone hot water bottle, which was now cold, from beneath the bed covers and carried it down stairs. I remembered pushing it down to the bottom of the bed last night but now it was time to fill it again for Mary, she may just appreciate it on a cold morning like this. After refilling it and placing it back into bed for her, I must admit to feeling like joining the stone bottle. Instead I went back downstairs and began to help myself to breakfast. Uncle Jim went off to work and left me by the fire that he'd lit before leaving. It was burning brightly but not yet giving out much heat so I huddled closer. After a while, I took a peep outside. It was really foggy and cold and made me feel more like staying by the fire. I didn't feel eager for work at all.

'Ruth, will you be all right?' shouted Auntie Lizzie from upstairs.

'It's a pea souper. Poor Uncle Jim having to drive the tram in this,' I called back.

'Don't worry love, he's used to it but you be careful.'

I sat by the fire again for a few minutes and warmed my toes. I just didn't feel like moving this morning. Grandma told me often enough not to put my feet so close to the fire as it caused chilblains, but I didn't know what chilblains were anyway, and Grandma was in bed. Picking up the poker, I jabbed it at the fire to make it burn brighter.

Going over to the door I opened it a crack again. I mean, it couldn't have changed from a few minutes ago but I was reluctant to move away from the fire. I suppose I lived in hope, but yes, it was still foggy and cold. It was an adventure walking in a fog, but it could be frightening too. It was so thick! You couldn't see a thing in front of you sometimes and it looked as if it was one of those days. Looking at the clock, I picked up my shawl and wrapped it tightly around me before I slipped into my clogs and opened the front door. I must set off now or I'd be late. Closing the door behind me I was soon enveloped in the fog.

Doris hadn't knocked, or if she did I hadn't heard her. Thinking that maybe she could have slept in, I called for her. As there was no response I realised Doris must have gone early this morning due to the weather. Wrapping my shawl even tighter around me I set off on my own. I could smell the fog and when it was a really thick fog like this it dulled the sound. Also, I must keep my eyes focused on where I was going as I couldn't always see where the road joined the pavement. I guessed I was going the right way but you could never be sure. I couldn't hear any footsteps made by the clogs from the workers. Perhaps I was late. My footsteps quickened. I heard someone coughing? Or did I? By now I was by the river as I could hear the water and it could have been a sound from there. I wasn't sure; I couldn't tell how far away people were either. I could hear another cough; maybe it was a man. They could be close, very close. Could it be someone I knew? Something was looming at the front of me…it was a lamp post; its light could hardly be seen in this thick fog. Then I felt someone touch my arm and I jumped with the shock.

'It is you, isn't it?' The voice sounded familiar.

'Oh! Billy…you frightened me to death.'

'Sorry! Come on then link my arm, I don't want to lose you.' He took hold of my hand and pushed it through his arm. I felt safe and felt my body relax.

'Do you think someone will see us?' I asked embarrassed.

'What? in this fog? Does it matter anyway?' he asked.

'Well! What will people think if they see me linking you?'

'It doesn't matter. What are you worrying about?' His face was close and I could see him waiting for my answer.

'It does matter really. I don't want them thinking the worst.'

'Oh! And what's that?' he teased.

'Well!' Ruth hesitated. 'They could think we're going together.'

'That's what you think of me?'

I was puzzled, 'What! I don't know what you mean?'

'You just said the worst is going out with me.'

'I didn't mean it.' We stopped under a lamp post and we stood looking at each other as the fog swirled around us.

'There's only one thing to do then isn't there?'

'What's that?'

'How about walking out with me then?'

'You mean go out with you?' By this time we were almost at the gates of the mill.

Turning towards me he bent over and kissed me lightly on the lips. 'Well! What do you think about it?'

'I think you're a very cheeky young man Billy Masters.'

'Does that mean no?'

'No.'

'All right then if that's how you feel…but I'm very disappointed.'

I could feel myself getting hot with embarrassment. 'But the answer is yes!'

He grinned. 'Come on lass, we'd better hurry or else we're going to be late and they'll close the gates and won't let us in.' We held hands and began to run. As we walked through the gates he rushed away and shouted, 'Wait for me when you've finished and I'll walk you home.'

Doris and Alice teased me all day after I told them about seeing Billy. I didn't mind though because I was in a dream. 'I can't wait until we've finished. I won't know what to say. What should I talk about?'

Doris laughed. 'I'm sure you'll find something to talk about, if it's only work.' I thought about that and went over and over in my mind how I would start the conversation.

'I don't know how to talk to boys.' I felt myself blushing at the thought.

'Then don't, there's other things you can do.' Doris winked at me.

'Doris!' Alice laughed.

'Don't tell anyone about my going with Billy will you? Keep it our secret,' I begged.

When the three of us walked through the doors of the mill that evening and across the yard we found Billy waiting for me at the gate to walk me home.

'Stay with me you two. I don't want to be seen alone with him, it just wouldn't do,' I begged.

We all walked slowly and chatted. I felt relaxed in his company as if we knew each other well. There was still the fog but now it was beginning to clear. It was still thick but at least we could see where we were going. When we passed a row of terraced houses Billy grabbed hold of my arm and pulled me towards the end house saying 'Look out for us girls.' He gently pressed me against the wall.

'Can I kiss you?' Billy asked.

I looked down at the floor with embarrassment and whispered 'Yes!'

Billy lifted my chin and pressed his cold lips onto mine. It was a cold night and our noses touched each other's cheeks…they were freezing. I wrapped my arms around Billy's waist.

'I'm cold, are you?'

'Yes I am.' He held me for a moment and I could feel the warmth from his body. It felt right but I knew my Aunt would worry if I was late.

'I'd better go; Auntie Lizzie will be expecting me.'

We joined Doris and Alice again and walked slowly to the corner of the street. Billy squeezed my hand before he left me then we both went our separate ways.

'What do you think of him Doris?' I wanted my friend's approval as I always had that special feeling for Billy Masters and now he was my boyfriend. I couldn't take it all in; could this really be happening to me?

'You're so lucky; he seems such a nice lad.' Doris sounded envious.

'I think he's lovely too. It's been a really exciting day for me, I can't wait to tell my Mam and Dad,' said Alice.

'What did he do when he took you away from us?' asked Doris.

'He kissed me Doris…on the lips.'

'Ooh!' they both echoed.

'Was he a good kisser?' asked Alice.

'I wouldn't know. I've never been kissed by anyone else, have you?'

'Only by my Dad when he tucks me into bed at night,' she answered.

I thought about that for a while. Seth had never kissed me but then again I felt glad about that. The very thought made me shudder. It must be nice to have a dad to kiss you goodnight and tuck you in that you loved. Maybe my Dad did that before he was killed but I couldn't remember. Uncle Jim didn't kiss me. I sometimes kissed him but it wasn't the same. Even though I loved him like a dad, I hadn't grown up with him.

After all the excitement, I hardly slept that night and went over and over those few minutes in Billy's arms. I felt glad to hear the knocker up's wire rattling on the bedroom window at five o' clock for Uncle Jim.

'Come on, gerr up' the man shouted, 'it's rainin' cats and dogs.'

I heard Uncle Jim and Auntie Lizzie get out of bed as the sound of people's clogs clattered down the street. Auntie Lizzie sometimes went back to bed for an extra half hour if she was still sleepy, so I waited until everything went quiet and thought at least it can't be foggy today if it's raining, so being eager to see Billy again I threw back my covers and got out of bed.

Chapter 5

I looked at the calendar. 'It's three weeks to Christmas.' I had been watching the calendar since the beginning of November and tried to prepare for it by saving any spare money I had.

Mary became excited. 'Please Aunty Lizzie, can we put up the tree…please.'

I remembered the very last Christmas I shared with my parents and brothers. It had never been exciting when Seth lived with us as there was never any money. If my Mam did manage to buy us anything then Seth managed to break or ruin it before we even saw it. I remembered my Mam making soup that last Christmas Eve ready for our dinner the following day but when we got up Christmas morning it was all gone. Seth brought his brother Uncle George home with him from the inn the previous night and they ate the lot. It was a different experience now for us at Christmas.

As soon as Uncle Jim came home from work and ate his meal, he was encouraged to bring up the Christmas tree from the cellar.

'Why is it always me?' Uncle Jim moaned.

'Because it isn't the place for any of us girls to go.'

'I suppose you're right,' Uncle Jim agreed.

'I know we're doing it earlier this Christmas. It's just that our Mary is getting excited and I don't think I can keep refusing her.' Auntie Lizzie said.

'I always get the dirty jobs. Women! Now I have four of them to contend with.'

Uncle Jim left the room to go down the cellar. I didn't envy him as there were spiders with their webs down there. I had been but only once out of curiosity. We could hear poor Uncle Jim banging about and cursing at the junk he was finding but he soon returned with the small imitation Christmas tree. It looked a little sad but after a good dusting he placed it on the sideboard. Auntie Lizzie set out the branches and then asked him to bring the ornaments also from the cellar. Uncle Jim could be heard cursing under his breath.

'I'm nothing but a slave to all these women. Do this, do that, that's all I hear.' I'm sure he could hear us giggling as he climbed down the cellar steps.

When he came back upstairs with the few ornaments he was covered with distemper dust from the walls. I pointed it out to him and he cursed again as I patted it off. We all thought it was funny. Mary had been playing in the sewing room after Auntie Lizzie told her she could have the scraps of material that she had left on the table in there, so when she appeared she was surprised when she saw us.

'Why are you smacking Uncle Jim's bottom Ruthie? has he been naughty?' she asked which made everyone giggle.

We carefully hung the few ornaments, some of them were a little tatty but still serviceable. They let me decorate the match boxes that had been saved over the last few weeks, to hang on the tree with a small sweet in each. It was something for Mary to look forward to. Auntie Lizzie told her she could have one of the match boxes off the tree each day in the last week before Christmas. She mustn't remove them herself but ask an adult to take one off the tree as the tree was old and very delicate. We finished off the tree with bits of cotton wool torn off a larger piece then stood back to admire it. It looked all right and Mary clapped her hands with pleasure.

It was the first time that Mary could really enjoy Christmas, as before she was too young. Now she was excited and Grandma and I began to prepare the streamers. While my Auntie cut strips of old newspaper, I made the glue from flour and water. Mary then pasted the end bits with her fingers, (she enjoyed that) and me and Grandma stuck them together. There was glue everywhere. Mary was full of it and the more we tried to clean up, the more things stuck to us. Finally, Uncle Jim stood on the step ladder and hung the streamers around the room. Mary really enjoyed making things and it made it more fun when we all did it together. I think it gave us a real Christmas feeling.

Mary had saved up a few pennies and put it with mine. I took out the jar and emptied the money on the bed and counted it. We found we had enough to go shopping for Christmas presents. I took Mary with me to Ashton, as it had more shops than Dukinfield. We had to find something suitable for everyone. We looked in the jeweller's window but it was all too expensive. Looking longingly at the gold lockets with chains, it was a shame but I knew I couldn't afford one. I imagined putting one around my neck and looking in the mirror but who would buy me one even if I would look after it. One thing's for sure, I would never take it off once I owned one. Maybe one day, I thought but not now. We spent a long time in Ashton looking round the market. Finding the right present was difficult. I put a lot of thought into it until I finally bought Auntie Lizzie a scarf. It was a pretty scarf and the green looked the same colour as her eyes. Uncle Jim was a problem. As he drove the trams, I decided on a pair of thin woollen gloves he could wear as he drove the tram to keep his fingers warm. I remembered him saying once that his fingers got cold. Grandma was easy. We bought her a nice purse for her to keep her pension in. When we returned home, we sneaked some old newspaper from the pile they kept for lighting the fire and took it up to our bedroom. Mary and I wrapped the presents and Mary helped by placing her finger on the first knot in the string then I could make the next knot tight to stop it from slipping. When I came to hide the presents under my bed, I found Mary had different ideas.

'I want them under my bed Ruthie,' Mary pouted.

'They're going under my bed Mary; I can look after them better there.'

'That's not fair.'

'It is, because I'm going to offer to clean the bedroom so they won't see them. If you want them under your bed then you can offer to clean the bedroom and I won't argue with you.' Mary didn't say much after that.

I went shopping alone soon after and bought a reading book for Mary, promising myself to spend time with my little sister to help her to learn to read. The book also had pictures which would help Mary understand. Again I wrapped it in old newspaper and placed it with the others under my bed. Mary wouldn't think of looking there for her present.

Mary became almost impossible to live with as it came closer to Christmas Day. She was so excited. Auntie Lizzie had to chastise her a few times. I was glad when it was the last week before Christmas then she could have one of the matchboxes each day off the tree. At least it was a small consolation. I was excited too as I had no idea what they had bought for me. I knew I'd have something but no idea what.

On Christmas Eve after supper, we all hung stockings on the string that hung across the large black metal fireplace (we used Uncle Jim's clean socks as he had the biggest feet). When we went to bed I told Mary to listen for the bells from Father Christmas's reindeer and sledge. Mary stayed awake as long as she could to listen for the bells until she finally fell asleep. Seth, my stepfather, once told me when I was young that there was no Father Christmas after I got up on Christmas morning and found no presents. After my disappointment I would make sure Mary believed in the Christmas story for as long as possible as believing in Father Christmas helped to make it magical.

When Mary awoke Christmas morning, she jumped out of bed and went to the window.

'What are you doing?' I asked.

'It hasn't snowed Ruth. It has to snow or it won't be special.'

'It doesn't have to snow for it to be special.'

'Yes it does. Aunty Lizzie said it weren't Christmas without it.'

'I suppose it does help to make it special but we can still enjoy it even without snow.'

Mary looked crestfallen so I went to the window and looked out. There wasn't a sign of snow, in fact it was raining and I had to admit that it didn't look like Christmas. It was a dark and dreary wet day but still felt cold. 'You never know Mary, it could snow.'

Mary cheered up a little then and I hoped with all my heart that it would. Auntie Lizzie called us to go downstairs. We weren't allowed downstairs until the fire had been lit and breakfast prepared but now it was all ready for us. Mary couldn't wait for the call and to see what Father Christmas had brought her.

As we made our way to the fire we could see the stockings were all full. We were allowed to look inside them before breakfast so we let Mary empty her stocking first and she had some colouring pencils, an apple and a bar of chocolate. Next, they all sat and watched while I emptied mine. I had fruit, a new penny, and a pen. Grandma was next and she had some new cutters for her pastry, Auntie Lizzie had needles, pins and a thimble, and Mary and I laughed when Uncle Jim emptied his stocking and found an onion and a potato. Poor Uncle Jim, we all thought it was funny and said that Father Christmas had played a trick on him but I guessed, knowing Uncle Jim that he did that himself just for fun, because he liked to make everyone laugh and be happy. After that we were allowed to open our other presents. Mary had a colouring book and a doll that Auntie Lizzie had clothed, and made an extra set so that Mary could change it when one lot got dirty. I had a writing pad and a bottle of ink for my new pen plus a new dress that my Auntie made, and it was very pretty with puff sleeves and a large white lace collar.

'You can wear it today Ruth, if you wish,' Aunty Lizzie smiled and I gave her a hug.

'Thank you Auntie, it's lovely.'

While Grandma Tyson and Auntie Lizzie prepared the lunch I played board games with Uncle Jim with the help of Mary. He was either no good at it or he allowed us to win until I let him win and he laughed when he realized what I'd done.

I helped to prepare the table with a clean white cloth while Grandma and Auntie Lizzie set out the cutlery. Grandma brought in the chicken from the oven in the fireplace and Uncle Jim began to carve it up. After he'd done that they brought in the roast potatoes and cooked vegetables. Sitting down to such a feast and sharing it with the family gave me an appetite. I thoroughly enjoyed the meal, especially when it was followed by my Grandma's home made Christmas pudding and custard. After dinner, as the adults were taking it easy to let their dinner settle, I looked through the window and noticed big snowflakes drifting past. I was excited knowing how much Mary wanted it to snow so I ran outside and shouted for the others.

'Look Auntie, I'm smoking,' I shouted as I breathed out and my breath was plain to see.

'Good job you're not,' answered my Uncle Jim, 'I'd give you a real clout if I caught you doing that.'

'Yes, and you'd have me and my Mam to deal with Jim if you did,' laughed Auntie Lizzie.

'It's snowing, look it's snowing. It's a special Christmas Mary.'

The grown-ups followed me to the door, standing, watching as the snowflakes stuck to the pavement, then we all went back inside the house.

'A 'ope it's not going to bi too deep,' Grandma said, 'as I have to go and 'elp Ethel tomorra.'

I watched the snow for a few minutes through the window. How things changed over time. I always loved the snow but it could get cold when you didn't wear shoes but those were yesterday's tomorrow's, I thought. I looked down at my feet then ran outside again and waved my arms trying to catch the flakes, but they all melted before I could show Mary who was fast asleep and missing it by now.

§§§§§

Grandma, Aunty Lizzie and Uncle Jim went upstairs to bed for a rest while I washed the dirty pots. They were reluctant for me to do it alone but I insisted. My mind was busy too, remembering past Christmas's. How my brothers would have enjoyed their Christmas here instead of with Seth. They never knew what a real Christmas was like. After I put everything away, Mary was awake so we put on our coats and went out into the snow. We began to make a snowman as the fall was sticking and becoming deep.

'Come on Mary, we'll go up the road where the canal is, there'll be plenty of snow there on all that grass.' We walked up to the grass and I wasn't wrong. The grass was on a hill overlooking the canal, but it wasn't too dangerous for Mary. We rolled the snow, and soon became aware of someone watching us. When I looked up I saw Uncle George standing on his doorstep from across the road.

I waved and shouted 'Merry Christmas Uncle George.' I felt sorry for him today, but only today, as he didn't really have a family to share his Christmas with.

'Why don't you come in the house Ruth and get a drink for your little sister. You must be thirsty too,' he added, 'and cold. You could warm yourself.'

'No thank you,' I called back. I felt very wary of him. Uncle George disappeared for a short time then appeared again in his coat and crossed the road towards us. I shivered but not with the cold. As he came close a snowball hit him. It was then I noticed a few boys climbing the hill from the canal. They began to throw snowballs at us and hit Uncle George again. It was Billy and his friends. I breathed a sigh of relief as Uncle George stopped then turned and went back to his house. I threw a snowball back at the boys. Soon a snowball fight was in progress. The boys were gentle with Mary, much to my relief, so I was the main target until Doris, passing by, joined us. After a short time she left but returned with Alice so the boys got a little more than they bargained for.

Billy began to chase me. I ran as fast as I could but he caught me and tried to rub snow into my face but I managed to stop him.

'What are you doing here anyway?' I asked Billy.

'Looking for you,' he replied. 'I talked them lot into joining me too.'

'I'm glad you did. I've enjoyed it. I haven't had a snowball fight for ages,' I said, 'and it was fun.'

By this time we were all a little wet and Mary looked rather miserable so I left them to take Mary home.

When we arrived home the adults were all up and wondering where we were. Grandma made a fuss and told us to change into dry clothes while she hung the ones we'd worn on any available space to dry.

'Just look at your new dress Ruth and your Auntie went to a lot of trouble making that.'

I felt terribly guilty. 'I'm sorry Auntie, I didn't mean to. It will be all right won't it Grandma?'

'Don't worry Ruth,' Auntie said, 'I didn't make it so that you'd be afraid to wear it. It will be fine.' I gave her a hug, she's so kind.

I sat and helped Mary with her reading book. There were times I stopped her in her reading to explain how to build up her letters. Mary became very frustrated in the end, closed the book and hit me on the head with it. While Aunty Lizzie lectured Mary there was a knock on the door and I went to open it.

It was Uncle Jim's brother Ted, Auntie Susannah and Peter. 'Surprise! Merry Christmas,' they said in chorus. 'I thought it would be nice to spend an hour or two with my big brother at Christmas,' said Ted. They took off their coats and Peter went to play with Mary, who cheered up when she saw him as he was only two years older and very patient with her bossy attitude. Auntie Lizzie lit more candles to make it feel like Christmas and we all played games then sang carols accompanied by Uncle Jim at the piano. Later in the evening the guests went home and we all went to church, except Grandma who was too afraid to walk in the snow in case she slipped and fell. We eventually arrived home exhausted and after a hot drink we all went to bed.

Chapter 6

Uncle Jim came home from work one evening with a newspaper tucked under his arm and a grim look on his face.

'The Titanic's gone down. There's supposed to be fifteen hundred people missing, presumed dead. I bet most of them were rich people. It seems that most of them were men too. It kind of makes you grateful sometimes that you're poor.' He threw the evening paper down on the table.

'What happened?' Auntie Lizzie said in alarm.

'There weren't enough lifeboats, obviously, and they said it was unsinkable…Huh! They made the women and children go first into the lifeboats. Damn shame for the men though. Makes you wonder if they'll ever get to the bottom of how many did go down with her. I can't understand it.'

'I thought it was supposed to be the best ship ever,' Auntie Lizzie said as she looked at the headlines in the paper, 'and it was the maiden voyage too wasn't it?'

'Aye, that's right. Like you say it was supposed to be the best so why weren't there enough life boats? How did it happen anyway? It beggars belief. Those poor kids. It's them I feel sorry for. Some of them won't even remember their dads.'

'Will you know anyone on there?' I asked.

'I don't think so dear, we don't know anyone who has enough money for that,' Auntie Lizzie replied.

'What's a titanic?' Mary asked.

Auntie Lizzie looked at her and began to explain. 'It's the name of a large ship where people were sailing to a faraway land. The Titanic was supposed to be one of the best and the rich people thought it was a special treat but it's sunk.' Mary was happy with that explanation and carried on playing.

'I bet there were a few diamonds and precious jewels lost on that ship,' Auntie Lizzie said.

'I bet there were…and lots and lots of money,' Uncle Jim said wistfully.

'It's very sad,' Auntie Lizzie added.

§§§§§§

It was Easter and the fair was visiting Daisy Nook in Ashton-under-Lyne so Doris, Alice and I decided we'd go. To save money we walked there instead of going on the excursion. Everyone appeared to be going in the same direction, excited children with their parents and young people with friends all looking forward to the fair and side stalls. It was a popular place to go for everybody. We couldn't afford to buy anything when we got there but we enjoyed walking round and watching other people enjoying themselves. Then I spotted Billy with a couple of friends.

'Hiya Ruth!' he called. 'Where are you off to?'

We walked toward the boys and they stopped to talk but then decided they'd walk with us for a while. Finding it too crowded to stay together; Billy suggested meeting up later before we went home. When they left us, Alice told me and Doris that she'd made a date with one of Billy's friends, Clem.

'You crafty devil, no one asked me for a date,' Doris said indignantly, 'and I must admit I fancied him too.'

'Never mind Doris, I'm sure you'll find another one.'

After that we were all on the look out for a suitable young man for Doris, which gave us a little amusement. They were either too tall or too small or she'd find something wrong with them.

Later, we met up with Billy and Clem and strolled home. Doris flirted with Clem but he seemed to be only interested in Alice. No one was eager to get home as we enjoyed each other's company. Billy gave me a kiss on the cheek before we parted and I made a fuss about it as I didn't like to show my feelings in public, it just wasn't done and Clem reminded Alice about their date the following week.

When the weather warmed up later in the year, Billy walked me home after work one evening and asked me if I would go for a walk after church the next Sunday with him.

'I can't really. I always go with my Auntie and Uncle.'

Billy looked disappointed. 'Oh well, never mind, maybe another time.'

'Maybe, you could just bump into us then perhaps you would be allowed to join us. What do you think?'

'What a good idea. You women are a crafty lot.'

'I'm already wishing I hadn't said anything now,' I laughed.

The next Sunday as I walked round the park with Aunty Lizzie, Uncle Jim and Mary, we saw Billy. He stopped to talk and sure enough, he was asked to join us by Auntie Lizzie. Billy fell into step with me and gradually hung back, encouraging me to join him.

'Is it all right Aunty Lizzie if we sit on the grass for a while?' I asked.

Auntie Lizzie frowned at me. 'If you wish, we will go to the children's swings soon so we can meet up there,' she added, 'and don't be long.'

'My Auntie's no fool Billy. I think she's guessed that this was all arranged.'

Billy smirked, 'I thought that too.' He placed his arm around me, 'It's nice to have you on your own though.' We lay down on the grass and talked. He tried to kiss me but I wouldn't allow it, not in the open where everyone could see.

After a while we walked round to the children's play area and joined the rest of the family. We passed the park keeper chasing a group of children and that took my mind back to when I played with my brothers here, and we were sometimes in trouble too. Mary was playing on the swings and Billy went to push her until I eventually took over. When Billy joined Uncle Jim and Auntie Lizzie on the bench, the conversation came round to decorating and Uncle Jim mentioned he had decided to whitewash the sitting room.

'I'll help you if you wish,' Billy offered.

'Have you done it before?' Uncle Jim asked

'No, but I'm willing to learn.'

'Right lad, you're on.'

Uncle Jim seemed much happier after that and so was I because that meant I'd be seeing more of Billy. It would be a new experience for Billy as all he'd done before was to be a labourer for his dad so he was eager to learn. He came round the following Monday and had tea then helped Uncle Jim scrape off the old loose whitewash. There was dust everywhere. It was in their eyes, nose and hair. Auntie Lizzie was not pleased when she found it escaping into the sewing room. The following day Uncle Jim showed Billy how to mix the new whitewash for them both to paint on. When it was finished and clean and tidy: we all breathed a sigh of relief.

§ § § § §

With my Aunt and Uncle's permission, Billy began to call for me on Saturday evening and we would go to the pictures if there was a particular one I wanted to see. The theatre was a good choice too and if there was anyone special appearing at the music hall like Vesta Tilley or George Formby who was born in Ashton-under-Lyne, then we would go to see them. Sometimes we had to travel a distance but it was all worth it. Billy liked George Formby and the way he would talk to the audience and Ruth would laugh at the way he would cough then make a comment about it. I admired Vesta Tilley too with her costumes and her way of pretending she was a man. If a singer asked them all to join in the chorus to their song, we would both join in and enjoy it. One day after watching Gracie Fields performing, I became really interested to join an amateur group, so I made enquiries but got cold feet when it came time to go.

Both Billy and I would go for walks if it was fine and he would treat me to an ice cream. Billy couldn't afford to take me out through the week because he didn't get much spending money, but as long as we were together it didn't matter to me but he insisted on only seeing me at weekends when he had a little money to spend.

'I would rather have money in my pocket when I go out with you. You deserve better than to be treated like a pauper,' Billy would say.

I wanted to see Frankenstein at the local picture house one Saturday evening so Billy took me and we sat on the back row. When it came to a scary bit I pretended to be afraid so Billy placed his arm around my shoulders and I buried my head into his chest. It was just an excuse for me to feel close to him.

Through the week Doris would persuade me to go for walks along Stamford Street if the weather was fine. It was the main street in Ashton and the place where boys met girls on summer evenings. As we walked up the street Doris caught sight of two young men walking towards us.

'What do you think of him with the checked cap?' Doris asked me.

'He has a nice face.' I replied.

As the boys reached us the one with the checked cap took it off with a flourish. 'Hello ladies,' he took a bow with his cap in hand.

Doris stopped. 'Hello.' I stayed in the background.

'And what do they call you?' he asked.

'I don't know if I should tell you,' Doris answered coyly.

The other fellow chimed in. 'His name is Sam and I'm Alfred.' He walked over to me, 'And you are?'

'Oh, it doesn't matter about me, I'm already courting.'

'Where is he then?'

'I only see him at week-ends.'

'What do you do through the week…die?'

The cheek of him. Who did he think he was talking to? I gave him a withering look. 'I go out with Doris.'

Sam was quick on the mark. 'Well, hello *Doris.*'

We sauntered along the street and round the corner towards a patch of grass. Alfred took off his jacket and placed it on the grass for me to sit on. After watching Alfred, Sam did the same for Doris. We all squeezed on to the boys' jackets and Alfred took a blade of grass and placed it in his mouth, chewing on the end. I watched him and hoped no one would see me sitting with him and tell Billy. I took off my hat and lay down, placing my head on Alfred's jacket and he followed suit. Doris and Sam were talking together so Alfred began to talk to me about his life and the family printing business where he helped his father and I found him really interesting, much better than I thought when we met. His father owned a small printers shop and Alfred helped him to run it.

'We're doing quite well really. It takes time to build a business but my Dad has been doing it for a while. He seems to be doing better than most.'

'What exactly do you do?' I asked.

'I do some printing. I make a good cup of tea too, that's the first thing I had to learn.'

'What do you print?'

'Anything really. We do printing and bookbinding. You know posters and special things for business people as well. Wedding invitations for those that can afford it. I'll take you round the place if you want,' he offered. I felt tempted as I often wondered how they printed the paper and forever curious as to how they ruled the lines but I hesitated. 'It's up to you, if you don't want to then that's okay too.' I shook my head.

'Do you rule lines on paper?'

'Yes, why?'

'I've always wondered how it's done.'

'I'll show you if you come.'

'You've talked me into it,' and I hoped that Billy would never find out what I intended to do. 'Does anyone know the time?' I asked because Aunty Lizzie didn't like me to be late for a meal.

Alfred took out a pocket watch from his top pocket. 'Almost four.'

'Anyway Doris, how about a date?' Sam asked.

Doris looked at me, 'Only if Ruth can come too.'

'Doris, I can't.' I felt so annoyed at my friend.

'Please Ruth;' she leaned over and whispered in my ear 'I'm scared to go on my own.'

'You'll join us won't you Alf?' Sam asked.

'Course, no problem.'

I gave Doris such a look to let her know in no uncertain terms that I wasn't pleased.

'How about next Wednesday? Have you already made previous arrangements?'

'Er…no,' replied Doris.

'Right then, we'll meet you here next Wednesday afternoon.'

It was a public holiday and I knew I wouldn't be seeing Billy through the day because he had already promised his mam and dad that he would help them decorate. He couldn't wait to show them his new skills.

Alfred looked at me. 'Is that okay with you?'

I nodded. 'As long as I'm home for tea.'

'I think we can arrange that,' Alfred promised.

We stayed a while longer but I grew even more agitated with the thought that someone would see me. I didn't want to upset Billy so eventually I sat up and prepared to go. Sam reminded us of the future date.

I didn't tell Billy about seeing Alfred as it didn't mean anything to me and I didn't want to upset him.

On the following Wednesday, Doris and I met the boys at the gates of Stamford Park. We walked through the park to the boating lake. The lads hired a rowing boat and began to show their skills at rowing. Sam almost went into the side at one point but after I became annoyed at the branches of a tree catching my hat and hair Alfred took over and managed to row us clear. After, we took a walk through the dingle and rested along the way but I was on pins hoping that no one would see me with Alfred. We all enjoyed it but I promised myself that as soon as Doris felt comfortable with Sam then I wouldn't go with them again. Also, I would allow Alfred to take me round the printing shop before that happened as the offer was too good to miss. As Doris seemed to be besotted with Sam, I didn't tell her what I intended to do so I met Alfred the following Monday evening alone.

'My Dad's working late tonight so you'll see it as it is.' He was very enthusiastic and I couldn't wait to see behind the scenes of the printing world and how it worked.

He took me into the printers and introduced me to his father, a sprightly man with greying hair and I watched in fascination as the printed sheets came out of the machine one after another.

'This is what I do.' Alfred took some of the printing letters and placed them so they were spelling backwards on a frame, then he packed them tight with something they called spacers. He showed me how they placed them on the machine and I stood watching mesmerised.

'Come on, I'll show you the machine that rules the lines.' He led me into another room and explained how it worked. 'These are the pens.' I could see them all in a row. You put the ink over there on to the pad you see above the pens and it soaks in. You feed the paper through so that as they pass under the pens the lines are drawn. We're not running this machine at present but I think you can grasp the idea.' I nodded.

He showed me the procedure of the book binding. How they printed the sheets, folded them with a folder (a small piece of polished whalebone) then sewed them together with cord before using fish glue to stick on the binding. He took me to the guillotine, a machine that was rather large and I watched as he switched it on and cut a ream of paper in half, in no time at all. I found it very interesting until he pretended the machine had chopped off his fingers but he was only joking. Before I left he took me into the house that adjoined the printing shop for a cup of tea. As we went through the hall, a wide hall with a marble tiled floor, I noticed the large curved sweeping staircase, the type that I dreamed about when I was a child. I smiled now at the thought of me sliding down the polished wood.

'Mum will be sorry she missed you but she had a previous engagement this evening.'

Alfred took me into the kitchen and made me a cup of tea. 'What do you think of my tea then? does it pass the test?' I nodded. 'Would you like to see the rest of the house Ruth?'

'What time is it?' I noticed the Grandmother clock on the wall. 'Oh dear, it's too late now. I watched Alfred's face drop with disappointment. 'Thank you Alfred, it's been lovely, and your house looks fascinating but it's time I went home.'

'I'll walk you home.'

'Thank you but no. I'll walk home on my own.' I didn't want to risk someone seeing me with Alfred and telling Billy.

When I went to bed that night I told myself I must stop seeing Alfred as it wasn't fair to either boy and although I liked him, I loved Billy. My mind in turmoil, I didn't sleep very well that night.

Having arranged to meet Alfred on the Wednesday on a double date with Doris and Sam, I kept my appointment. Doris didn't really need me as it was obvious she felt comfortable with Sam. Alfred held my hand then tucked it into his arm.

'Mum says that you must come to tea Ruth as she would like to meet you.' He stopped and for a moment he looked into my face. 'Have I ever told you what beautiful blue eyes you have?'

'Get away with you. You sound like the wolf from Red Riding Hood. Let's walk.'

'Well you have…honestly.' We walked a few steps then Alfred stopped again and turned to her. 'Will you come to tea?'

'I can't Alfred. I've told you I already have a boyfriend.'

'But what about me?'

'I like you but I love Billy. I did tell you when we met.' He stopped walking again and turned to me.

'I'm sincere.' He stood for a while as if battling with his thoughts. 'Can I change your mind?'

'No Alfred, I'm afraid not.'

'What should I tell my Mother?'

'Can't you tell her we had words and I won't be seeing you again?'

'Do you mean that, honestly…won't you see me again?' Alfred put his arm around my waist and drew me to him, and the thought of stopping him never entered my mind. 'You can't blame me for this.' He pressed his lips onto mine and although I intended to struggle if this ever happened, I found I couldn't. I knew then that if I hadn't met Billy it could have been a different story.

When Alfred left me that evening, I could see he was upset and I cried myself to sleep that night. The following morning I felt as if a heavy load had lifted from my shoulders and looked forward to seeing Billy the coming week-end.

When Billy and I next went for a walk we passed a poster and I stopped to look at it. The printers were Alfred and his father and I felt proud that I knew how it was printed but I didn't tell Billy. The poster advertised a local dance.

'What are you looking at that for?' Billy asked.

'I like dancing and just wondered where it was.'

'I've never been to a dance and I don't fancy it either.'

'Why?'

'I'm just not interested.'

It wasn't mentioned again until they were on their way home from work the following Friday.

'I'll call for you tomorrow so you'd better have all your finery on ready.'

I didn't understand. 'What do you mean my finery? Where are you taking me?'

'Where do you think? To the dance of course,' he replied.

I spent a long time getting ready that Saturday evening and put on my favourite suit. Auntie Lizzie made it for me months before and I was really fond of it so wore it on any special occasion. I did my hair differently and took great care with my appearance. Then my thoughts went back to Alfred. What if he came to the dance? What would I do? If he did I hope he doesn't ask me to dance or I don't know what I'll do. Billy could suspect something and what would I say? When I opened the door to Billy after his positive knock I found him looking very smart in a suit I hadn't seen him in before. He wore his hair freshly greased and combed back.

'You look handsome doesn't he Aunty Lizzie?' I commented as I took him into the kitchen.

'You don't look so bad yourself either,' Billy grinned.

'I won't be a minute; I'll just get my wrap.'

I ran upstairs and came down to join Billy. As we went through the parlour I heard Auntie Lizzie talking to Uncle Jim.

'They make a lovely couple don't they Jim,'

'Aye, our Ruth could do much worse than Billy.'

I felt glad that both my Aunt and Uncle approved of Billy. I loved him so much, I don't know what I would have done if they hadn't liked him.

When Billy and I entered the room where the dance was being held we were both surprised at the number of people already there. He wouldn't dance and he watched me instead as I danced with people I knew.

As I danced I saw a familiar figure enter the room. It was Alfred and our eyes met. I was dancing the Barn dance and hoped he wouldn't join in. I couldn't imagine how I would feel with his arms around me again. My wish was granted. He didn't join in but stood and watched my every move instead. My legs felt wobbly as I made my way back to Billy.

'Come on Billy, have a dance with me,' I asked.

'No, I'll leave it to you,' he answered and sat quietly for a while, then my worst nightmare happened and Alfred came and asked me to do the waltz.

I couldn't really refuse; it would have been awkward so I allowed Alfred to lead me to the floor. 'Why are you doing this Alfred? I've told you how I feel.'

'I know, but surely you can't refuse me the chance to have an excuse for putting my arms around you just this once.' I hoped that no one suspected anything. I could feel my body tremble when he held me. Billy watched me and Alfred intently as we danced around the room. Why did my body let me down like that? That didn't happen when Billy held me, but then again, I was accustomed to Billy holding me. When Alfred took me back to Billy, I felt very guilty.

The next dance Billy claimed, thank goodness! Now I knew why he didn't like dancing, he had two left feet. By the time we finished my feet felt bruised and sore after he'd stepped on them so many times. I didn't ask him to dance again and when he took me home that night, he told me I was invited to his house the following day.

'My Mam wants to meet you so she said to come to tea.'

§§§§§§

I walked to Billy's house. It was a lovely day. The sun was shining and there wasn't a cloud in the sky. I made a short cut through a small park. There were birds singing and twittering and some of the Sparrows were arguing, as Sparrows do. It seemed a perfect beginning to what promised to be a pleasant occasion. There were children playing in the trees at hide and seek and it took me back through the years when I played with my brothers...until the park keeper chased us.

Although nervous at meeting his family, I was looking forward to getting to know everything about Billy. His home was a small, middle terraced stone house on a small street with terraced houses facing each other and all with small gardens at the front with a gate. A waist high wall surrounded the gardens and Billy's had large shaped stones placed on the top. The house was not as big as the one I lived in, but in the street the children and dogs played freely to the sound of steam trains passing by, just like my own home, and I knocked timidly on the front door.

Billy opened the door and after taking my coat, introduced me to his Mam and Dad. They made me very welcome and his Mam went into the kitchen to make the tea. We had tinned salmon with bread and butter. His Mother opened the tin of salmon as a treat.

'You must be someone very special if she opens a tin of salmon for you,' Billy's dad said through the puffs coming from his pipe.

'Shut up you silly devil,' his Mam looked embarrassed then added; 'I'm opening a tin of fruit and cream too. What about that?'

'It's coming to summat,' his dad said through another puff of smoke. 'I'd better get some overtime in.' He looked at me and winked. After that day I became a regular visitor.

In the following weeks I would sometimes see Alfred outside my house, leaning on the railings of the embankment talking to Sam while they waited for Doris. Trying hard to avoid him I would wait until they all walked away but at the same time I was inquisitive to know if he had a girlfriend. On occasion he would surprise me by being there when I stepped outside the house and would come over to speak to me. He was always polite and I couldn't find it in my heart to not spend a little time in conversation. He always found something flattering to say to me and when Auntie Lizzie was introduced to him once, she said later she found him charming but I still loved Billy.

When I next saw Doris, she told me that Alice didn't go out with Billy's friend Clem anymore. Soon after I saw Doris, Sam and Alfred stood across the road. Trying to avoid embarrassment, I waited for them to disappear before I ventured out. I was surprised when they were joined by Alice. From the front window of the house I watched them walk up the street and felt a pang of jealousy, which shocked me, when I saw Alfred and Alice hold hands.

Chapter 7

Saturday evening, there was a knock on the door and Auntie Lizzie went to answer it. I heard muffled voices then Auntie walked into the room followed by an older woman that I didn't know. Uncle Jim stood up and his mouth gaped open.

'Auntie Hilda!'

'Let me sit down, my feet are killing me,' and she flopped into the nearest chair which Auntie Lizzie had just vacated.

'Where's Arthur, is he on his way?' Jim looked at the door.

'I'm on my own.'

'What are you doing in these parts?' asked Uncle Jim. There was a long pause before Hilda found her breath.

'Did you hear about the Titanic?' Auntie Hilda asked.

'That was a bad 'un,' Jim's face looked solemn. A lot of lives were lost that night.'

'I lost Arthur…everything…well, enough anyway.'

'You were both on it?' asked Auntie Lizzie with surprise.

'Oh yes, unfortunately, but there weren't many men survived it.'

Mary interrupted them. 'You must be a rich lady.'

Auntie Hilda laughed, 'Not as rich as I was…who is this child?'

Auntie Lizzie laughed. 'Not mine…well not by birth but she lives with us now. This is Mary.' She nodded to me, 'and this is her sister Ruth but the rest of their family; our Betsy—my sister—two boys and second husband perished in a terrible house fire.'

'Oh dear! So you have what's left of them, that's sad and after…?'

'We do indeed.' Placing her arm around Mary, Auntie Lizzie added, 'and we're very proud of them too.' Mary looked up at Auntie Lizzie with a self satisfied grin.

Uncle Jim interrupted. 'What happened with the boat anyway? It was an iceberg so they say but surely someone must have seen it coming.' Uncle Jim was obviously curious.

'Seemingly not. I think many of us were a little inebriated and it was almost midnight you know. It wasn't spotted until it was too late and then we were doomed.'

'It was the maiden voyage wasn't it?'

'It was and it was a beautiful ship. Sailing was a pleasure until then.'

'It must have been terrifying,' Auntie Lizzie broke in.

'You'll never know how much. I never want to go through something like that again. I'm afraid a cruise is definitely out from now on.'

'I can understand that.'

'It's funny but I couldn't wait to get on it, and then I couldn't wait to get off it. Those poor people who couldn't get off must have felt terrible. When you think that they paid all that money to sail from Southampton to New York and then that happened.'

'Paid a lot of money…to die,' Uncle Jim said.

'Well…yes.'

'What brought you here then?' asked Uncle Jim.

Auntie Hilda coughed and looked very uncomfortable. 'After the Titanic went down and took Arthur with it, I was heartbroken and dazed…still am. I can't believe it happened. I watched all those people who jumped into the water. Some of them drowned immediately through the cold and some were swimming before they disappeared. It's not right! I still expect Arthur to walk through the door but it isn't to be.'

'You poor thing,' Aunty Lizzie looked sad.

'After that I realised just how much my family meant to me. Arthur went down with the ship you know…he was my best pal…my life.' She dabbed at her eyes. It was awful as we sat watching that boat disappear and knowing our loved ones were on it. I couldn't believe he'd gone. Still don't. I still believed he'd walk through your door then Jim, when you asked for him.'

'It must be difficult for you.' Uncle Jim looked grim.

'I kept watching the water expecting to see him swimming towards us. I looked and looked for him but of course he'd gone.'

Uncle Jim cleared his throat. 'I know you were devoted to each other.'

'Yes, we were. There'll never be another like him.'

'Maybe not…but, well, you're still young an…'

'Jim!' Auntie Lizzie said firmly.

'It was so cold that water. Even those who jumped in and started swimming…' she stopped for a while and wiped tears from her eyes, 'most of them didn't make it.'

I went into the kitchen and put the kettle on.

'So…' Uncle Jim cleared his throat again, 'I hardly recognised you when you came in. We haven't seen you for…well…since you married Arthur and moved up in the world…' he frowned, 'have you come to stay?'

'I knew I could depend on you Jim, you were always a good hearted sort…and you Lizzie.'

'Well, you're more than welcome Auntie Hilda but we can't possibly offer the same as you've been used to,' Auntie Lizzie looked surprised.

'And I wouldn't expect it dear.' Auntie Hilda snuggled into the chair she was sat in and made herself more comfortable. 'You've no idea how good it feels to be with family again. I've been like a lost soul…and by the way, don't call me Auntie. Let's face it, I'm not much older than you Jim and Auntie does make me feel old.'

'How long do you think you'll be staying then?' Uncle Jim asked.

'Really Jim, you shouldn't be asking her that. Especially after what she's been through' scolded Auntie Lizzie. 'It doesn't matter.'

'I only wondered…'

'Be a dear and bring my luggage in Jim. It's on the steps outside.'

Uncle Jim went out and came back with two cases. 'I don't know what you have in here but it weighs a ton.'

'Oh dear, and I'm hoping you'll take it upstairs for me too.' Hilda grinned.

'Women!' Uncle Jim grunted.

'I'll get Ruth and we'll start on the bedroom straight away then you can go to bed whenever you're ready. You must be tired out. Sorry we can't offer anything better, but it's the best we can do. Come on Ruth.' Auntie Lizzie went to collect dusters and I followed her to help her with everything else before going upstairs. We cleaned my bedroom and prepared it for her.

'Come on, let me show you your room and Jim will bring up your baggage.' Auntie Lizzie left the room to go upstairs followed by Auntie Hilda, and I followed on with her handbag.

It took her a while to climb the stairs as she was rather fat.

'These stairs are really steep; I'd forgotten how steep they were,' she gasped.

When we eventually went inside the bedroom, Auntie Hilda threw herself on the bed and looked around the room. Sitting up she remarked, 'It'll do, its fine. I can't wait to go to bed tonight I'm so tired. It seems a life time ago when Jim's Dad and I were young and living here and you still have some of the same furniture too.' Her fingers stroked the chest of drawers at the side of the bed.

'Yes, it's been very serviceable.'

'Well you've obviously looked after it Lizzie, Auntie Hilda added.'

'I've done my best.' Auntie Lizzie looked pleased.

We made our way downstairs then and while Auntie Hilda was eating her supper, my Grandma came home from Ethel's.

I went to put the kettle on to make my Grandma a drink and she followed me.

'Who's that?' she whispered.

'It's Uncle Jim's Auntie Hilda,' I whispered back.

'What's she doin' 'ere?' Then Auntie Lizzie came into the kitchen.

'I'll finish off now Ruth, you see to Auntie Hilda.'

Auntie Hilda was finishing the food and drink she was given, and then sat back.

'I enjoyed that. Is this your mam?' she asked Auntie Lizzie.

'Yes, she lives with us since my dad died.'

'That's nice.' Auntie Hilda yawned. 'I'm afraid it's my bed time. 'Nice to meet you,' she said to grandma then went upstairs to bed.

I wasn't long after that. I made my way upstairs to share Mary's bed. She was already asleep so I tried to be quiet and carefully got into bed and snuggled into her.

'Ruth you have cold feet,' she murmured but went back to sleep immediately. I lay a while unable to sleep but eventually dropped off.

The following morning Auntie Lizzie & Grandma gave us breakfast. 'I wonder what Auntie Hilda is going to do,' Auntie said.

'Should I take something up for her?' I asked.

'You can go and ask her if she would like a cup of tea but I don't like anyone eating in bed unless they're ill.'

Auntie Hilda did want a cup of tea. I took it up to her and found her sat up in bed with her hair in a long plait. When she went to bed the previous night her hair was in a bun on the top of her head so I showed surprise.

'Are you getting up for your breakfast Auntie Hilda?' I asked.

'What time is it?' Auntie Hilda looked at her watch on the side table. 'Oh yes, I'll be down after my cuppa, thank you child.'

I thought about Beth and how she brushed the hair of her mistress.

'Would you like me to brush your hair Auntie Hilda?' I asked.

'What a dear! I'd love you to brush it for me.' Auntie Hilda got out of bed, rummaged in one of her bags and brought out a hair brush. Sitting on the edge of the bed she asked, 'Can you manage if I sit here?'

'Yes thank you,' I said as I kneeled on the bed and took the brush she offered.

I brushed her hair until my arm ached. 'Is that all right now?'

Auntie Hilda took the brush from my hand. 'That's fine Ruth and thank you very much.'

I would have loved to see Auntie Hilda do her hair and watch how she could get it into the neat bun she wore yesterday but I wouldn't be rude so I left and ran downstairs.

As I cleaned up in the kitchen, Auntie Lizzie took out a small plate from the cupboard and began to cut a piece of bread.

'Can you prepare the table for Auntie Hilda please? Just put the cloth on the end where she's going to sit.'

When Auntie Hilda came down for her breakfast, her hair was in a bun and looked neat and tidy again. Auntie Lizzie gave her a boiled egg with a slice of toast. When Auntie Hilda finished it she thanked them wholeheartedly.

'That's the best boiled egg I've had for a long time and I really enjoyed it. I slept well too.' Going over to Grandma she gave her a hug. 'I'm sorry I wasn't very friendly last night but I was very tired.'

'It's okay,' Grandma replied, 'they've explained why you're 'ere an' I'm very sorry.'

Auntie Hilda sat and talked and told them all about their Ford car, which hadn't been driven since Uncle Arthur's death. She also added that she doubted if she would ever drive it. Her voice went quiet as she told us of Uncle Arthur's work and the people he worked with. All about London and the friends she and Uncle Arthur made there. We all listened in amazement as she spoke about their rich friends, their houses and servants; both of her friends and her own.

Of her servants she said, 'You have to give them their duties and tell them that cleanliness, regularity and neatness are the rules of the day. If you do it yourself sometime then you have a good idea how long those duties take. If they need you to be watching them all the time then they're told to go and you employ someone else.'

Auntie Lizzie coughed and said, 'I don't think we will ever have any problems in that area.'

Auntie Hilda carried on, 'Cooks are important. They mustn't be wasteful and they must cook the food properly. Also, their cleaning is important as dirt is the enemy. Everything must be spic and span and that goes for all the staff. You must treat them fairly, and hopefully they will respond.'

Auntie Hilda was a fun lady who bubbled with enthusiasm over the least thing. Everything they did together was something they would remember. In the street she would join the children at skipping, not that she could do it very well, and other street games too, she was never afraid to 'show herself up' like most ladies. One of the boys who lived on the street came out playing with a hoop and stick.

'Hey lad, can I have a go?' she asked.

The boy grinned and passed it over to her and Auntie Hilda ran down the street as best she could while they all gave her their support. Even going to the park was special with her as she never tired of pushing the swings and she would allow them to go up high. Mary had lots of cuddles from her and I loved to cuddle Auntie Hilda too as she was soft and squashy. Also, she was very generous and would take us shopping, buying us little gifts too, which were very gratefully received.

Billy was in awe of Auntie Hilda and would sit fascinated as she talked of her life. I went out with Billy at week-ends but through the week Auntie Hilda would fill my evenings.

Taking us to the pictures felt good as she always insisted on buying sweets.

'You can't go to the pictures without sweets; it's like having a bath with no water,' she would say and we laughed and loved her to bits.

We had help with the housework too. Nothing seemed to get Auntie Hilda down and she was always willing to roll up her sleeves and get 'cracking' as she put it, not even shirking at cleaning the lavatory outside. When I went to bed I would sometimes hear her crying but said nothing as I gathered Auntie Hilda missed Uncle Arthur an awful lot.

One Saturday evening Auntie Hilda was playing Ludo with us and it was getting close to our bed time.

'Do you know I just fancy a glass of beer. Does anyone else feel like coming with me?'

Uncle Jim and Auntie Lizzie looked stunned.

'You don't want to go to the inn Hilda, decent women don't go there,' Uncle Jim said with disgust.

'You're wrong Jim. This woman wants to go and I'm not indecent so why shouldn't I?'

Uncle Jim went quiet for a while. 'I don't fancy taking you.'

'Oh c'mon you old fool. I'm not going to show you up and get drunk.'

'If you insist but I don't like it.' Uncle Jim went to get his coat while Auntie Hilda went to change her clothes.

'Are you coming Lizzie?' she asked.

'No she's not.' Uncle Jim answered for her. 'That's something I won't allow.'

'It's okay Hilda,' Auntie Lizzie added, 'I don't think I would enjoy a drink anyway and then there are the children.'

'Surely Grandma would look after them.' Auntie Hilda tried to coax her.

'No. You go and enjoy yourself. It'll make a change for Jim.'

They were gone a while and when they returned I wakened to the sound of Auntie Hilda singing and laughing. I crept out of bed and stood at the top of the stairs listening to what they were saying. Uncle Jim didn't sound too pleased but I could hear Auntie Lizzie laughing.

The following morning I asked them if they enjoyed their visit to the inn and Uncle Jim told us all about it.

'This woman can't part knock it back Ruth. She put me to shame…and do you know how much she drank?'

I shook my head. 'No.'

'She drank three pints,' Uncle Jim looked disgusted, 'and then I absolutely refused to get her anymore. Talk about the demon drink…this woman just thinks it's another name for it.'

'Spoilsport!' Auntie Hilda remarked before she added, 'Anyway, how can it be bad when it makes you so happy?'

'No kidding Lizzie, she sat with me and the men and swapped jokes. Mind you they were all clean.'

'I'm glad about that,' Auntie Lizzie frowned.

'I almost had to drag her out of there and the fella's were asking when she was going again. I told them…never!'

While Auntie Hilda was with us I hated having to go to work and found it a real chore. I felt I was missing something. When she decided to go back home she first went for a walk but didn't tell us it was a walk to the shops.

When she returned she had a full bag of goodies of things my Auntie could never afford.

'Go and check I haven't left anything as soon as I've gone, but not now as I can always pick it up next time.'

When they waved her off and went upstairs to check as she had asked, they found gifts for them all. When she bought them, nobody knew. There was material for Auntie Lizzie to make dresses with beads and sequins, books for me, a doll for Mary and a new shaving brush for Uncle Jim because she noticed he needed one as his bristles were getting sparse. Auntie Hilda said she missed London but we all missed her because when she left she left a large hole in the family.

I began to write her letters and after a while Mary added one too.

Chapter 8

August 4, 1914, war broke out.
The headlines in the morning paper screamed:
GREAT BRITAIN DECLARES WAR ON GERMANY

Billy said he'd join up but his parents and I did our best to persuade him not to. The German army were on the march and they were taking over. One day Uncle Jim picked up the paper and read it out. 'Germans use asphyxiating gas to gain ground near Pyres.' I was filled with horror, thinking of Billy and the boys we knew who had gone off to war. I felt thankful that Billy hadn't joined up yet and still held on to the hope that his plans would change. He would have signed up at the beginning of the war and even been willing to lie about his age if he had to but he'd put it on hold.

No one thought it would last longer than six months at the most anyway, so it surprised everyone when Christmas came and went and it was still raging. When the newspapers began displaying the headlines of what the lads were suffering it made everyone realise that it was far more serious than they had first anticipated.

I pleaded with Billy not to join up and I thought he was listening to me but he joined up as soon as he could. His Mother and I still tried very hard to talk him out of it but he wouldn't listen. He signed up without telling us his plans and before long he left.

I felt annoyed but when he came home on leave I did think he looked very smart in his uniform. All the same it upset me a lot. Uncle Jim kept bringing the newspaper home every evening to read out the headlines. He would unfold the paper and read them out loud to anyone who showed interest. Even when we ignored him he still read them out loud.

Neutral shipping was warned to stay away from the waters surrounding us and Ireland, because of the submarines. 'This is serious,' Uncle Jim said as he refolded the paper and placed it on the table, 'it's going to affect our lives a lot.' We didn't know what to expect and we lived in fear of the unknown.

That's when the truth really sank in with the family. This war was threatening to our everyday lives. Food would be in short supply for a start, as if that wasn't bad enough. Every able man was leaving and many of the unfit attempted to sign on the bottom line but were refused. They did need every man to fight but there were other ways the disabled could do it. Some could work on munitions. Life continued with more recruits leaving to fight the war and Billy couldn't wait to join them at the front. Things were really getting bad. Women were taking men's jobs and much to everyone's surprise, they were good at them. Women in service were leaving for the factories and better wages. It brought a freedom for the women they had never known before.

Anyone with a garden put it to good use by growing vegetables or keeping hens or ducks for the fresh eggs. If they had the room they kept both poultry and grew vegetables. Grandma spent a lot of time with Ethel now as Ethel needed a lot more help owing to her arthritis.

Billy kept writing to me and telling me how impatient he was to 'Get to them Germans,' but each time he wrote I breathed a sigh of relief, knowing that he was safe in his home country. Finally, he had his orders for France and came home for a few days before he left.

When he called for me I flung myself into his arms. 'I suppose I'm proud of you Billy but I would much rather have you here to hold me close when I need you.'

'We'll make the most of these few days. I'll see you every evening and dream of you every night,' Billy promised and I laughed.

In those few days Billy and I pushed it to the back of our minds about the war. He would wait for me to finish work and walk me home. Occasionally we would go in the park and talk of our future and of what we had to share. It was quiet there and there were no interruptions. He spent time between my house and his so that his parents would see him as much as possible too.

His leave soon came to an end, and I worried about him going to the war in France. It was his last night and I was saying goodbye to him on my doorstep before he went home to his parents. He was leaving first thing in the morning and it broke my heart.

'I'll be home again before you even miss me.' His cheeky grin made something stir inside me as it always did. I touched his hair and pretended to move a strand from his forehead. It was an excuse really; as I just wanted to touch his hair once more before he left me again.

'I know we've known each other a while but we haven't really got to know each other yet,' I frowned, 'and already, you want to leave me.'

'You're kidding me Ruth Lewis, you know me very well, and you know you do. I want to go to war and protect the people I love…like you.' He squeezed me tighter. I pulled away, 'All the same, you must be fed up of me or you wouldn't want to go.'

'You know that's not true. The sooner everyone joins up, the sooner this bloody war will be over. I'd like to think I helped to make it safer for you.'

'I suppose I'm selfish but I want you to stay here with me. I'll miss you so much Billy.' I couldn't stop the tears from running down my face even though I promised myself I wouldn't cry.

'I'm glad because I'll miss you too.' He attempted to dry my tears with his fingers. 'There's so much I want to share with you Ruth…and I will, don't you fret. We'll get married when it's all over and then there's the children we'll have. Maybe a boy for me and a girl…for me,' he smiled. 'We'll soon see the end of this war. You'll see.'

'I hope you're right.'

'And don't you go looking at other boys while I'm away.'

'Oh Billy, as if I would. Anyway, I would have thought you knew me better than that.'

'I'm just reminding you.'

'And you don't go falling for some French girl either,' I added.

'There's no worries there Ruth. There'll always be only one girl for me.'

We kissed for the very last time and I didn't want him to go. As he walked away he pushed a little package into my hand.

'This is for you. Keep it close to your heart and never take it off.' I was curious and began to open it but he placed his hand over mine to stop me. 'No,' open it when I've gone. I'll write as soon as I can, and I'll write as often as I can too. I hope you'll write to me the same.' I nodded. He walked away and as he turned to go round the corner, I followed him. The tears filled my eyes again as I watched him walk up the street until he waved for the last time before he was out of sight. With a little sob I ran back to the house. Would I see him again, I wondered. I couldn't bear it if he was killed.

Closing the door behind me I didn't speak to anyone as I was too upset, but ran upstairs to my bedroom for privacy and to open the tissue that surrounded my present. When I did open it I found a jewellery box and inside was a gold locket and chain. It caught at my throat as I remembered telling him once how much I always wanted a gold locket on a chain. He'd remembered and bought it without saying a word. I thought back to when I said it then realised it was when Mary almost drowned. Fancy him remembering from then. It must have cost him a fortune, a fortune he didn't have. He must have been saving up for a long time. When I opened the locket there was a picture of me and Billy inside from when we were in Blackpool on a trip. Also in the tissue was a card. On the card it read, 'I know you always wanted one of these so I've taken the liberty of not only buying one for you but placing our pictures in it too. He signed it Billy, then underneath, 'Together forever.' Turning it over I found a poem that he'd written out for me. It read;

You have my soul, you have my heart.

You have my mind, and if we part

an invisible cord no one could sever,

will keep us both 'Together forever'

I sobbed as I placed the locket around my neck. Taking my special angel box from the chest of drawers, I opened it and checked my reflection in the inside mirror. The gold locket looked beautiful but I looked terrible. Fondling the ebony box, I held it close to my heart. This box was a special gift that my Grandma gave me when I first came to live with them. There was a beautiful painted angel on the front with the sky and clouds behind it.

'This is yours Ruth, just yours. It's a special box that my Mam gave to me when I was a girl. You can put all your secret things in there because no one else is allowed to touch it.' Grandma made me feel really special that day and it helped. Now I would use my box for something very special. I emptied the bits and pieces from inside and carefully replaced them with my card from Billy. I picked it up again and read it as if I had never seen it before then I placed it back inside the box and closed the lid. Fancy him writing a poem. I didn't know he had it in him. I took the poem out to read it again. Did he write it or was it copied. No, it was too personal to be copied, he must have written it himself. Placing it carefully back in the box, I decided that all Billy's letters would go in there for security. I placed it back in the drawer and lay on the bed listening to my Auntie and Uncle talking downstairs while the tears escaped from my eyes.

'Should I go to her Lizzie?'

'No Jim! Leave her, there's nothing you can do for her.' It went quiet for a while. 'What's the matter now?' asked Auntie Lizzie.

'Some use bringing the paper home when I can't even read it.'

'And what's stopping you?'

'How can I read that with our Ruth upstairs all upset?'

'Don't you go up to her. I'm afraid it's not you that can stop those tears.'

'Actually, I've really been thinking of signing up. It's been on my mind for a while now and I think I should…'

I heard my Auntie raise her voice. 'Don't you dare Jim Vale. I don't know what you're thinking about. What will happen to us? Have you thought about that?'

'I don't want to listen to you complaining anymore. I think it's time I did... for King and country and all that you know.'

With those words ringing in my ears, I started crying again. How could Uncle Jim go to war? Life was getting unbearable. This war had to end soon. I decided to go out somewhere, anywhere, to keep my mind busy. I was sick and tired of the war. People didn't talk of anything else and it was time it was over. I dabbed at my face with my handkerchief then went down the stairs. Uncle Jim's paper was still showing the front page. Bending over to read it I found I could only read a little of the article 'Battle of the Somme.' Then the tears filled my eyes again.

'Where are you going Ruth?' Auntie Lizzie sounded concerned.

'Just out. I feel that I need the walk.'

'Don't you think it's a bit late dear?'

'I know it is but I just want some fresh air.' I walked out of the house.

It was late and I knew it was past my bed time but I really needed the fresh air. First of all I walked across the road and stood looking through the fence at the top of the slope that led to the river below. Watching it as it rushed on its way it made the noise feel comforting. I thought at least there are some things that never change. I could see the white of the foam it made as it hurried towards the sea. I watched the water and thought about Billy and when Mary went missing. He was just a boy then and now he's a soldier and off to war in those few short years. Tears began to run down my cheeks again and a small sob escaped me. Looking up at the moon, I wondered if Billy could do the same when he was in France. Maybe he's looking at it right this minute in Ashton. A sudden warm feeling spread through my body. Then I heard someone singing from behind me so I turned my head. It was Uncle George and he came over the road to join me. He looked the worse for wear so I began to walk away. As he came close he tumbled into me.

'Hello darling, where are you going?'

'For a walk.'

'I'll come with you.' Uncle George attempted to walk in step with me but I hurried all the more.

'What are you rushing for?' his hand held my arm.

I didn't feel as if I could be bothered with him right now; he did try my patience at times. 'I'm in a hurry,' I answered.

'Why? To get away from me?' he asked.

I could never be rude to anyone but tonight was different. 'Yes!' I said as I shook my arm free.

Uncle George got the message and turned away. 'Bitch,' I heard him mutter to himself. Breathing a sigh of relief, I walked on but my Uncle must have crept up behind me as he unexpectedly wrapped his arm around my neck and pulled me round to face him.

'Give your Uncle a big sloppy kiss.' His grin looked evil in the half moon light. He tried to force me to kiss him and I struggled. He was strong and held my face with his fingers, digging them into my cheeks with a grip like the bite of a lion. I couldn't escape, and then he kissed me. There was no one around to help me and I couldn't get out of his hold. I could feel his fingers hurting me as he kissed me hard and long. Finally he let me go. I wiped the spit from off my mouth with the back of my hand and felt contaminated.

'That'll teach you to say no to me. Remember that in the future because you might not get away with just giving me a kiss next time.' I hated him in that moment. The last person to kiss me should have been Billy, not Uncle George. My despicable Uncle had taken advantage of me. How dare he? I hoped it wasn't a warning regarding Billy. He must come home to me. He had to do. Oh God, please keep him safe, I prayed.

As Uncle George walked away, he swaggered up the street and I felt afraid of him and sick. I could feel my lips begin to bruise and swell. What had I done? In the future I would think twice about taking a walk at night alone, especially when Uncle George was around.

§§§§§

One Sunday evening Uncle Jim tried to talk about the war but Auntie Lizzie and I refused to listen as we didn't want to give him ideas about signing up. He kept quiet about it all night but later he started talking about it again. I went into the kitchen to make a drink of tea and he picked up the paper from the table and began to read it out.

'Jim, will you stop it?' Auntie Lizzie called. 'Please don't go to war. Do you really want me to live through hell?'

'Sorry Lizzie but we all need to do our bit or who knows what could happen. If everyone had your attitude then the war would soon be over…and we'd all be prisoners…if we lived.'

All Uncle Jim could talk about in the evening was war, war, war, and how much he wanted to sign up. I felt depressed with it all as the newspapers were full of it and everyone else seemed to talk of nothing else. All I wanted was normality and Billy home but it was a long time before that would happen I guess, if at all.

The next night Uncle Jim came home with the evening paper and I read it myself.

'What with the zeppelin raid and the ships being sunk and the bombs being dropped, it just goes on and on.' I pushed it aside. 'When will this bloody war end?' I said in disgust.

'Ruth, there is no need to swear,' my Aunt reproached.

I picked up the paper and began to read it again. It was all about heavy fighting and what our troops had captured. They were making progress but all I wanted to read was how near to the end of the war. That was what everyone wanted to read.

'Ruth, put that paper down.' Auntie Lizzie asked. 'You'll only upset yourself.'

Uncle Jim took it off me and began to read it to himself.

The following morning I received a letter from Billy.

Chapter 9

Dear Ruthie,

We arrived in France on Sunday morning, and after disembarking, marched six miles to the camp. The weather here isn't as hot as I expected. We are under canvas. We sleep on a board floor with one blanket. It suits me perfectly! I never slept better than last night.

A motor lorry caught fire this morning and all the troops were fallen in to assist in extinguishing it. However, the fire was soon put out without the assistance of the immortal 126 boy! Me, in other words.

The crossing of the channel was fine! France is 160 miles from the post of embarkation, and I stayed on deck all the time. Did the voyage affect me!

We had an enthusiastic reception from the French people. The food here is quite good.

It has just started raining and it looks as if it's going to turn ugly, yet I am thankful to say, I am in the pink of condition. One needs a constitution of iron to stand the tough life out here.

I can't say too much of what is happening as letters are censored. Give my best to your Grandma, Lizzie, Jim and a big kiss for Mary. I miss you all but mostly you my love.

See you before not too long, I hope!

Love Billy X X

P. S.

I hope the locket is close to your heart as it's the only thing that's keeping me going here.

I tucked the letter away in my angel box as I hummed to the tune of 'Meet me tonight in dreamland,' and wondered what Billy was doing at that moment. Would he tell me what was happening or would he be afraid to worry me? Knowing Sam also joined the army about the same time as Billy, I didn't see him or Alfred again. Alice was also another I lost touch with but I thought that was for the best if she was seeing Alfred. I still saw Doris but didn't have much time to spend with her after Billy left. I'd given a lot of thought to changing my job. Doris and Alice didn't come with me this time but I felt that I had to do something that would help my Billy.

'I've noticed they're getting closer. It's going to be our turn next,' Auntie Lizzie commented after reading the evening paper.

'We'll be all right Auntie,' I said as I hugged her, 'don't worry.'

It was worrying and we lived in fear of what our future held. How many of our men were going to die? how many men that we knew? There were already neighbours and their sons who had perished in the trenches mostly and we all wondered who next?

Applying for a job as a fettler in a factory, I felt I was helping Billy by working on munitions. It wasn't a nice job but someone had to do it! I didn't mind as long as I focused on him. The following day I had a letter from Billy as he did promise he'd write whenever he could.

After reading it over and over I opened the angel box and placed the letter inside with the other, I tucked it into the top drawer in the bedroom away from inquisitive fingers. Mary could read well and I didn't want to share my letters with anyone else. They were mine…all mine. At night I took them out of the box and slipped them under my pillow. I hoped it would make me dream of Billy. If it didn't, at least I would feel closer to him. As I lay there one night in the quiet of my bedroom I wondered how Billy was feeling and what he was thinking. I missed him so much. The moonlight came through the curtains so I threw the blankets off me and got out of bed again. Going to the window I looked up to the moon. Is Billy looking at it now, I wondered. Even in France he could see the moon so maybe he was looking at it this very moment. I stood there for a while and hoped he was, and then went back to bed feeling much better.

Uncle Jim applied for the army but was rejected much to Auntie Lizzie's relief. He always insisted it to be his duty but at last we were all reprieved from the worry. His reading the paper out loud stopped and he curtailed his talk of the war. He was obviously disappointed. After pay day I made up a parcel for Billy and sent it with a letter. Mary also wrote a postcard for him. I packed them up carefully. If he missed me as much as I missed him then he was suffering.

The war still raged and one morning I had another letter from Billy and a letter from Beth, Uncle Jim's sister who was much younger than Uncle Jim and whom I was very fond of. I opened Billy's letter first.

Dear Ruth

Life here is hell and there isn't a better word for it. It's wet, muddy and the stench is unbelievable. I don't think I shall ever forget it for the rest of my life.

Thanks very much for the parcel, it's splendid! The famous 'sweet' brand of cocoa is much appreciated by all my comrades. I make a canteen every evening and they all declare it to be the best cocoa they have tasted! Does this cocoa meet with appreciation two miles behind the firing line within range of the German shells!

I'm afraid I have shaved my head and you wouldn't recognise me. I did it to keep the little blighters away (lice). Still as handsome as ever though!!!

I am glad to hear of Jim's rejection by the recruiting officer. I feel sure it is all for the best! War is a rough and dangerous game and he is better occupied looking after his wife and family than stopping German bullets. Nevertheless I still hold to the opinion that he is strong enough to be a soldier!

The weather here has changed, mostly rain and lots and lots of mud but I'm trying to make the best of it.

Thank Mary for the pretty postcard. She is getting on fine with her handwriting.

I miss you Ruth and I hope this war will soon end then we can be together again. Please write often as I look forward so much to your letters and news from home.

Love
Billy X XX XX

Then I opened Beth's letter.

Dear Ruth

Hello my favourite niece. How are my brother and the rest of the family? Thought I'd let you know that I have now become a mother. I gave birth to a baby daughter three months ago. I've only just begun to get into a routine so that's why I haven't written before.

I wondered if you would like to come and stay one week-end with me and Percy and Joan our baby girl. We could catch up on our news and you can see the house too. It's lovely having our own place and the rent is very good. Come and see how the other half live ha ha.

Write soon.

Love Beth

I felt thrilled for them. They were a lovely couple and so much fun. It would make a nice change for me staying a weekend with them, and would take my mind off worrying about Billy. I wrote back and made an arrangement for me to go at my first opportunity which was the following Saturday. Lizzie hurriedly made a dress for Joan, and I went out to buy her a present.

When Saturday came, I arrived home from work, pushed down a little food and prepared for the journey. Having packed most of my things the previous night I was soon ready, but when I went to catch a tram I'd just missed one. Calling into a tea room I found the tables were full then Mrs. Harding, the doctor's wife spotted me and beckoned me over to her table as she was sitting on her own.

'Please join me Ruth. How are you coping with this horrible war my dear?' she asked.

'How is anyone coping with it? My intended is away fighting and I worry myself to death about him.' Mrs. Harding's covered my hand with hers.

'I know how you must feel my dear. Our eldest son Clive is also away and he's on the front line.'

'Like my Billy,' I added.

At first I felt a little shy with the doctor's wife but as we had so much in common I soon relaxed and we were in conversation like old friends.

'You must come and see us sometime Ruth…and let me know how your Billy is, and I mean that.' I thanked her.

As I got up to go I turned to Mrs. Harding. 'I shall carry the hope for their safety in my heart, and may God keep them safe for us.'

As I walked towards the tram stop I thought about the doctor and his wife. They were very good to me and Mary after the fire, bringing clothes and food to help things along, but now this war had brought everyone to the same level. It didn't matter how much money or high esteem they held, we were at war and feelings were all the same, to keep loved ones safe and free from harm. God must be very busy listening to all our prayers. Then another thought went through my mind. What about the enemy? Their families must also be praying for their safe return. Why did they all want to fight each other? They didn't know the people they were fighting; they could be wonderful people…so why fight them to the death as they did?

I must stop thinking like this.

Beth and Percy lived a walk from the tram stop so I had a way to go. It was beginning to rain so I hastened my steps. There were children oblivious of the weather still playing on the streets with their hoops and other games and some of them wore no shoes. It brought back the memories of my own childhood and the first pair of boots my Auntie bought for me. When Auntie Lizzie told me she was taking me to Ashton for a pair of boots I was so excited and I never stopped talking all the way to the shop where she bought them. I felt so thrilled with them and walked home with my head bent and my eyes on my boots until my Auntie Lizzie told me to look where I was going or else I'd soon fall. I would have settled for a pair that didn't fit properly but Auntie made sure they were right for my feet. I was so proud. It was the first pair of shoes I had that was bought for me specially, at least in my memory.

A little boy with a cheeky grin looked up at me and brought me back to reality. It made me wonder how my brothers would look if they had grown to be men. When I turned on to the street where Beth and Percy lived, I was relieved. Besides being weary with the walk I was also rather wet.

Beth and Percy's house was a small two up two down in a long terrace on a small street, but spic and span. Their front doorstep was freshly stoned and the windows shone. Their furniture gleamed with polish and everything looked well cared for and smelled fresh. A vase of Marigolds took pride of place on a dining table covered with a chenille cloth, their golden colour cheering the room.

'Oh Ruth, it's so nice to see you after such a long time. Let me look at you…you're very wet.'

'I know. You can always rely on the rain when you have a long walk.'

'Would you like to go and change?'

I nodded. 'If you don't mind?' As Beth took me to the bedroom I asked. 'Have you pressed anyone's shoelaces lately?'

'No, thank goodness,' Beth laughed her beautiful, unforgettable laugh. 'Mind you I have many worse jobs now with the baby and everything.'

'I've missed you,' I said and meant it.

'Fancy you remembering about the shoelaces from when I was a maid for those horrible people.'

'I remember a lot of things. Brushing your ladies hair and pulling it on purpose if she wasn't nice with you. Some memories I have that maybe I shouldn't remember.'

'Like what, or are those your little secrets?'

I didn't pursue that. 'You do amuse me at times Beth.'

We hugged each other then Beth went downstairs. I stripped off my wet clothes and rummaged through my bag. I put on a comfortable frock that I wouldn't worry about if the baby made a mess of it, and then I went downstairs. Going over to the crib I looked inside. The baby looked back at me with the most gorgeous big blue eyes.

'Oh Beth, she's beautiful. May I pick her up?' Beth stood smiling. Her face was full of pride as she nodded. I picked up the baby with great care. She was a beautiful child with those lovely deep blue eyes, a small amount of fair hair and a wonderful smile. Somehow, Beth had managed to find enough hair on the baby's head to put in a ribbon and it looked so cute. I sat the baby on my knee and cuddled her, and looked forward to the day when Billy and I had a child that I would hold like this. I was reluctant to pass her back for Beth to feed her. After the baby had been fed she went back in her crib and slept while we girls talked until Percy came home from work.

Beth and I went into the kitchen to prepare a meal for us all while Percy sat and read the evening paper as best he could amongst the laughing from the kitchen. Beth kept her eye on the time as she was very aware of when the baby would need feeding.

In the evening, after we washed and tidied away the dirty crockery, Beth tried to show me how to knit as she was making a little knitted jacket for Joan, the baby. I gave her the little dress that Lizzie made for Joan, also a rattle, hair brush and comb that I'd bought. After thanking me, Beth looked at the clock and excused herself to breast feed the little one. I tried not to watch Beth as it was embarrassing but I felt curious so took a little peep when I could and wondered how it felt to have a baby suckling you. It was an experience I couldn't wait to have. It was lovely having a baby to hold and I held her as often as I dare without Beth getting annoyed. Joan was a lovely child and so sweet natured.

When I went to bed that night I lay and thought of Billy again. Would we ever have our own house like Beth and Percy? It seemed a life time away. Would I make a good mother? I was sure that Billy would make a good father but a lot would depend on me. I hoped that I would cope. I didn't get as much sleep as usual with the baby needing feeding through the night, and as she was teething her cries were prolonged,

Pushing the pram to the local park the following day, I stopped at the corner shop for a few sweets. It gave me a boost and the idea of how it would feel to push my own child and it also gave Beth a much needed rest. I walked proudly around the park and when someone asked about the child, I pretended I was Joan's mother. When I arrived back at the house, Beth was beginning to panic as I was a little late for Joan's feed but as the baby seemed happy enough, I was forgiven. It was a lovely week-end that we all enjoyed and I promised I would visit again when I was asked.

After I returned home, I decided to learn to knit. A woman at work taught me and soon I knitted my first pair of socks, men's socks. After packing them up in a box I wrote to Billy.

> Dear Billy,
>
> I've learned to knit and after losing my mind (and my stitches a few times) I have at last done it. I almost gave up but I thought of you and persevered. I have actually managed to knit these socks ready for your first winter away. I don't want you to feel the cold and hope these will keep you snug and warm.
>
> I've followed the fighting in the newspapers and hope that God will keep you safe. Please look after yourself and come home in one piece to your family and me. I miss you so much.
>
> Love you
>
> Ruth x xxxx
>
> P. S.
>
> Saw our doctor's wife the other day and she told me that their son was also fighting on the front line. He's called Clive Harding if you come across him.
>
> P. P. S.
>
> I wear your locket close to my heart and always will.

Chapter 10

As the war seemed to be never ending and the Zeppelins were bombing London frequently, I decided to learn first aid. Soon after, I saw Doris and told her about the first aid classes so Doris said she would come with me. When Doris called for me to go, I was surprised to find Alice was joining us too. It was like old times as we walked up the street laughing and giggling as we did in the past. I didn't ask about Alfred and his name was never mentioned.

The army band came round the streets every night playing rousing marches and banging a drum loud enough to split your ears. The recruiting sergeant encouraged young men to follow them.

'You get a free pint of beer when you arrive at the barracks and a regular wage too so why not sign on the dotted line lads. Your country needs you.'

Jobs were very few and men couldn't get regular jobs so there was no money for tobacco and ale. It wasn't much of a challenge so there were many following to join up. Their neighbours urged them on to follow, especially those with family who were already away fighting.

Soon the Canadian soldiers and Australians began to appear. Not much later and advertisements were seen asking for more women to work on munitions. Factories were making shells and one in Ashton made TNT. Mills were working full time making much needed cloth for bandages and uniforms. Someone was overheard to say, 'At least the war has given us jobs.'

The Germans planned for the war and seemed to march quickly through Europe. There was no food on the shelves in the local shops and milk was sold in a powdered form. Sugar was substituted with saccharine tablets and the cakes were fatless. Those with their own gardens were lucky because they could grow their own fresh vegetables. Farmers seemed to be okay too so if you were lucky enough to know one then you wouldn't do too badly either.

Others found even some apple pies didn't contain apples, it was Swede with saccharine to sweeten. Everyone adapted well, didn't complain much but just got on with it. Struggling through was second nature to them anyway. Then I received another letter from Billy.

> Dear Ruth
>
> Thank you for the socks, I shall wear them with pride knowing that your own hands knitted every stitch.
>
> I'm feeling very sad today because after the 'morning hate,' I lost my best mate John; he got a bullet. They shot him in the head so he didn't have much chance. It was a sniper and I only wish I could get hold of the #?#!#. If you're wondering what the 'morning hate' is, it's named because we fire haphazardly at the enemy lines and whatever the reason for doing it, it doesn't part release some tension but I hate this war. I hate the Germans. I hate everything to do with it and can't wait until it's all over and my time's up for coming home. At present I'm living in a dug out with no candles and rats galore. No home comforts for us.
>
> Through the day movements are restricted as their snipers and lookouts are watching us all the time and wouldn't hesitate to take a pot shot at us and that's how John came to die.
>
> Can't wait to see you again.
>
> Your ever loving and sickened
>
> Billy

When I read his letter I cried myself to sleep that night, poor Billy and poor, poor John and his family. I prayed to God to keep Billy safe and bring him home.

In June the following year, Mr. Murray from next door, who was much younger than his wife, unexpectedly came home from the war after being wounded in the trenches, so I went to see him. Mrs. Murray had been a bad tempered neighbour, always shouting at the children for one reason or another but over the years her temper had cooled, and we girls had gradually learned to get on well with her. When Mary and I were young Mr. Murray would sometimes shout to us when we played outside.

'Shuddup you noisy kids.'

After a few times of this Mary called him Shuddup. I remembered how Mary, when she was a little girl and playing in the big back would suddenly come rushing into the house.

'Whatever's the matter?' I would ask.

'Shuddup's come home,' Mary would answer. I smiled to myself at the memory as I knocked on the door.

I heard Mrs. Murray shout 'Come in,' so I entered.

'HiyaShuddup,' I said when I saw him lying on the couch. This brought a smile to his face. 'How are you?' I asked.

'Hellish!' he answered.

'Sit down Ruth,' Mrs. Murray urged, and I sat on the closest dining chair.

'Don't sit there Ruth,' she waved to an easy chair, 'sit on that one, it's a lot more comfortable.' I stood up and moved to the easy chair that was offered. It was shabby to look at and well worn but still comfortable. Realising how weary I felt I snuggled into the feather cushions.

'What happened then Mr. Murray?'

'What didn't happen?'

'What was it like there?'

'Hell! No other words can explain it better.'

'My young man is on the front line and I wondered how bad it was.'

'He's in the trenches is he?'

'I believe so. Is it really bad?'

'It's bad. There's death everywhere, even when you're not under attack. I suppose I shouldn't tell you really but mostly there's constant shellfire which kills you whatever you're doing.'

'Aren't you protected at all?'

'Call it what you will but when there's a shell-burst near you, you don't have much chance.'

'I thought the trenches protected you.'

'Not enough sweetheart and you daren't peep over the top to see what's happening or a sniper's bullet'd get you. Come to think of it you didn't need to peep over the top and a sniper's bullet could still get you.'

That worried me and I hoped Billy wouldn't be a target. 'Were there a lot of injuries?'

'Aye, there was that…and then there was the disease and the rats.'

'You poor man. I bet you're glad to get home. At least it's reasonably safe here.'

'Aye, it feels good to be clean again. Them lice really get to you.'

'It must have been awful.'

'It was. When the only entertainment you have is to run a lighted cigarette down the seams of your shirt to watch the eggs squirm and shrivel, it has to be bad. Of course you could squash the lice between your thumbnails but they can't part breed quick.'

'Uggh! That's terrible.' I then noticed a far away look in Mr. Murray's eyes and felt that he'd had enough of talking.

'Would you like a cup of tea?' asked Mrs. Murray

I nodded and got up to go into the kitchen with her.

'He's really suffered you know Ruth.'

'What is his injury?' I asked.

'It was a shell, it's shattered his knee. I doubt if he'll ever walk again but at least I've got him and not everybody can say that about their men folk.'

'That's true; there are so many not coming home.' I thought about Billy and hoped he wasn't going to be one of those.

'I know, and he told me about them rats, especially the brown ones, they were really feared. He lay injured and when he came round they were all around him. If he hadn't have screamed, bringing attention to himself, he fears that they would have finished him off. He must have been near death. He tells me the rats ate the dead soldiers given a chance and them rats were everywhere. The trenches were running with them. He has terrible nightmares.'

When I left the Murray's house I felt sick and my head ached so I went upstairs as soon as I got indoors and opened my Angel Box, reading yet again the letters from Billy and I read the poem again too.

You have my soul, you have my heart.

You have my mind, and if we part

An invisible cord no one could sever,

Will keep us both 'together forever'

As I read the letters, my hand reached for the locket around my neck. It wasn't there. I felt all around my neck but the locket and chain were missing. Jumping out of bed, I looked around the floor then under the pillow and under the bed. It wasn't there. Running down the stairs I began to look around the floor, chairs, kitchen as I felt panic rise into the back of my throat. It wasn't to be found anywhere.

'What on earth's the matter?' asked Uncle Jim.

'I've lost my locket. Have you seen it, has any one seen it?' I asked.

Auntie Lizzie came into the room with Grandma and both shook their heads but went back into the kitchen and began to search everywhere. They searched the shelves and even the cupboards, heaven knows why I thought, but there was nothing left unturned. No one found the locket and I began to cry as I disappeared upstairs and flung myself back onto my bed. After I sobbed for ages, I lay looking at the ceiling and wondered what Billy was doing at that moment. How I wished I could see him. Was losing my locket a bad sign? What if I never found it again? He must have saved up for it for a long time and I've lost it. I bet he'll be mad when he knows. I won't tell him until I have to. It may just turn up. That thought settled me for a while.

When I went downstairs again, Auntie Lizzie tried to console me.

'It'll turn up love, you'll see. I'm sure you'll find it Ruth. It can't be far surely. When did you last see it?' she asked.

I thought for a while. 'When I had a wash this morning, I remember feeling it around my neck. I've felt it since but I can't remember when. I've been thinking and thinking about that but I just can't remember.'

'I'm sure you'll find it Ruth.' Auntie Lizzie repeated. 'Don't worry.'

When I went to work the following morning, I kept my eyes mostly on the floor as I searched for the locket. It could be anywhere. It must have come undone and dropped without me even knowing. That hurt. How could I not know when I lost something that meant so much to me? One of the men saw me looking around.

'Lost something Ruth?'

'I've lost my locket. I just hope it'll turn up.'

'If I hear of anyone finding one, I'll let you know.'

I thanked him and as I walked away there was a loud explosion. It felt as if the building was falling down. All the windows blew in and the broken glass flew everywhere. I ran but I didn't know where I was going. It was chaos everywhere. There was dust, glass and everything wasn't in its usual place. I could smell and taste the dust. I thought the Germans were attacking us. I could feel blood running down my face but it didn't hurt so I gathered it wasn't serious. There were people who were injured and I looked around to see if I could be of help to anyone. People were running blindly, like scalded cats, not really knowing where they were going just as I had a few minutes before. The labourer whom I had been speaking to was badly injured and there were a couple of men helping him. I realised just how lucky I had been.

I could see people bleeding wherever I looked and after a while, Dr. and Mrs. Harding appeared from nowhere and were doing whatever they could, even if it was only to comfort some of them. Mrs. Harding asked me to help her with the casualties and while we were helping the wounded she told me that her son Clive had been killed. I also found that he had a younger brother who had been sent to the front line too and I felt the pain for her. Everyone came out of work early that day. As they were expecting another blast, most made their way to the cemetery because of the open space. Eventually, they heard that it was an accident that happened in Ashton at the TNT works. People in the street outside the works were killed and there were children coming home from school among them. Even a child swimming in the baths died as the blast shattered the glass roof above her. There were many made homeless and the blast affected homes two miles away.

Finally, everyone made their way home, if they had one to return to, to find their families. I found on arriving home, there were no windows in the house and two of the gas mantles had blown. Uncle Jim was nowhere to be seen and we waited anxiously for his return, finding out later there had been a road block that stopped him. Auntie Lizzie bathed my head and confirmed it was not a very deep cut but needed something on it anyway so I allowed everyone to fuss over me for a short time. What a relief that no one in the family had been badly hurt, although I felt sorry for those that had.

After we all sat down to eat, Grandma Tyson prepared to go out.

'Where are you going Mother?' asked Auntie Lizzie.

'On'y round corner. Al 'ave t' go an' see mi friend Ethel. I dunna know 'ow this'll 'ave affected 'er an' shop. If she's okay a won't be long.'

All the neighbours were stood in the street talking in groups about the explosion and everyone seemed to be trying to outdo each other with their knowledge.

It was getting late and Grandma Tyson still hadn't come home so Auntie Lizzie began to worry.

'Jim, can you help me look for my Mam. I don't like her being out as late as this.'

'I'll come with you,' I said.

'No dear, you stay in case she comes home and needs something. She'll be tired.'

They went out into the night and I looked through the window for my Grandma. An hour later a neighbour brought her home after finding her sat on a bench in Ashton. The neighbour told Ruth that when she asked my Grandma what she was doing there she said she couldn't remember and when the neighbour suggested she went home Grandma said she couldn't remember where she lived. I thanked the neighbour before she left.

Sitting my Grandma down, I went into the kitchen and made her a cup of tea.

'There you are Grandma,' I said as I gave it to her. 'Would you like something to eat with it?'

Grandma looked at me strangely. 'Whor is it?'

'It's tea. You like a cup of tea don't you?'

'Do I?' Grandma looked vacantly at me. 'I do.' Grandma began to slurp it. 'Where do ya live?' she asked 'and wha 'r you called.' I sat down quietly at the side of her. 'Am cowd,' Grandma shivered then turned her head round and looked into space. 'Stop chunnering,' she said angrily to an imaginary person. I worried. When Auntie Lizzie and Uncle Jim came home they showed concern too.

The following morning Grandma Tyson worsened and we couldn't understand what she was talking about. Auntie Lizzie told her to stay in bed and she would call the doctor.

'I'm afraid it's not good news Lizzie. Your Mother's quite ill.' Dr. Harding looked very serious, 'She hasn't long. All you can do is keep her comfortable.'

The following day Grandma Tyson died. Her funeral was the day before the mass funeral of forty-seven bodies from the T.N.T. explosion. I wrote to Billy and told him all the dreadful news but didn't tell him that I'd lost his locket.

It was a sad time for the family and all the people involved regarding the TNT explosion. Grandma Tyson's funeral was private with not many people there and when I returned home, I climbed the steps to the front door. It didn't seem that long ago when my Grandma kneeled on these steps and showed me how to use a donkey stone. She had her own way of doing things and insisted I did them the same way.

The following day the church was full of mourners after the explosion. There were many tears shed that day with many broken hearted family members.

'As if we haven't enough with the war without all this going on. Where's God when you need him?' asked Uncle Jim.

'Don't blaspheme,' Auntie Lizzie scolded.

A month later the postman brought me another letter from Billy.

Dear Ruth

Sorry to hear your bad news. I always liked the old lady. What a shock it must have been too when you heard the blast of the T.N.T. and how drastic to lose so many people in one go. I'm just glad that you're safe.

Sorry again but I asked around and nobody knows Clive Harding. What rank is he?

Last night about seven in the evening, we heard the sharp cracking of rifle fire mingled with the rapid tap tap of machine guns. This lasted for about half an hour. It appears that the Germans were attacking our lines. They were driven back with heavy losses. When you receive my letter you will have heard of the French successes in the champagne district. As I have often thought the grips of allies is tightening. I believe that we shall clear the enemy out of France and Belgium but at a great cost and after a long period of increasing effort. The war is a long way off its end yet, notwithstanding the optimistic reports of journalists. Nincompoops! The great bombardment has ceased for a while in our district at least.

Take care of yourself for me and look after your family. If you could go and see my Mum and Dad I would be grateful.

Love you lots and miss you so much.

Love
Billy X XXXXX

I read it many times before I placed it carefully in the angel box with the others. How much I missed him he would never know. He also didn't know I was already going to see his parents at least one evening a week, it made me feel closer to him somehow.

Two of our neighbours had telegrams to tell them their husbands had been killed and my heart went out to them. Their screams on hearing the news would forever stay in my memory. Although some of the young children had forgotten their dads, they were still upset because of how it was affecting their mothers. Some of the older women who lost their men folk found themselves in the workhouse, as without their husband's support they couldn't cope.

I heard tales of the workhouse and they weren't pleasant. Someone told me it was tougher living inside them than living outside and the place was grim, full of disease and with a shortage of food. I was also told that they searched you, stripped you, cut your hair short and made you wear horrible clothes.

Men, women and children were all kept separate which wasn't nice or fair to families. It was desperation that sent you to the workhouse and I hoped it would never happen to me or mine. I lived once near to starvation before the fire and I didn't want it to happen again, not ever.

I read the latest headlines:

22 NOVEMBER 1917 'GREAT VICTORY'

British troops, aided by the fine work of the tanks, have penetrated German defences to a depth of five miles, captured many villages and strong points, and taken over 8,000 prisoners. I couldn't read any more so I pushed it away.

A few weeks after Christmas food rationing began, after the German submarine blockade. Now there were restrictions on sugar and meat. Luckily with Grandma's training both me and Auntie Lizzie knew how to get round these cut backs and would still provide meals for us all. It was a small price to pay after what our men were suffering.

In my letter to Billy I told him all about it but agreed that it would seem nothing with what he must be eating. I did my best to write to Billy regularly, telling him all the news, which must have been boring with all he could see but he said it was like a breath of fresh air receiving my letters. At first I was dubious about telling him about Clive but after second thoughts I told him. After all, he didn't know him.

Billy didn't send me a letter for a while but maybe it was because he couldn't get them through.

The weather began to turn colder and I couldn't help but feel that the war couldn't go on much longer. Everyone began to feel mournful and depressed. It didn't seem right. Maybe Christmas would bring good news. I felt optimistic. After I wrote yet another letter to Billy I went to post it, then on to see his Mother and Father. His Mother met me at the door and I could see by her face she was upset and had been crying but I was invited in as usual.

'What's the matter Mrs. Masters?'

'I'm sorry Ruth...here.' She passed me a telegram. I could feel my heart start beating faster and it felt as if it would come through my ribs as I read the words.

WE DEEPLY REGRET TO INFORM YOU THAT WILLIAM MASTERS IS MISSING, BELIEVED KILLED.

...I fainted.

Chapter 11

The house was on fire and I was suffocating. I could see my Mother and brothers fighting to get out and I couldn't help them, but it wasn't our old home, it was Aunty Lizzie's. This house was much larger compared to our old home and I saw the six steps to the front door which I counted every time I climbed them when I was a little girl.

My Grandma was on her knees donkey-stoning the steps. I could see the mud scraper near the front door and looked down at my shoes. They were odd just like they used to be and I realised my feet were small again. I shouted to Grandma to help me get my family out of the burning building but she wasn't listening to me but kept on stoning the steps. I climbed the stairs to the three bedrooms but when I got to the top, I was back downstairs and going through the three rooms there. It was when I began to go down the steep steps of the cellar and went through a spider's web that I woke up with a start. My dream was so real and I had been a child again. I sat up wet with sweat, and wiped my face on my pyjama jacket. Lying back again I recited part of the poem Billy had written; 'and if we part, an invisible cord no one could sever, will keep us both 'together forever'

I said that to myself over and over again. Did he know this was going to happen? Did it mean that he was still alive? I didn't feel he was dead but was that my being optimistic? I didn't know anything anymore.

Although I still went to work, through the motions of living, there was a continual dull ache in my chest. There was no enthusiasm for anything any more and I could see my Auntie Lizzie felt worried for me.

'Our Ruth is looking poorly lately Jim. She's just a shadow of her usual self. What do you think?' I heard Auntie Lizzie say to Uncle Jim.

'She'll sort herself out Lizzie, stop fretting, our Ruth's not an idiot.'

'Men!' Auntie Lizzie muttered under her breath. 'You never seem to understand what we women go through.'

'We're just practical, that's all. We still feel, but don't air our thoughts like you women.'

'Huh Men!'

A visit to the Doctor and his wife was my first priority. 'They made me very welcome and served tea as I told them about Billy missing. Discussing the war with them and how it started brought the memories back.

'What happened to your son?' I asked. 'Do you know?'

'He was asleep it seems and there was a shell fired. It was a direct hit. He never knew anything about it, or so one of his men told us. What happened to your young man?'

'I wish I knew. It's the not knowing that really gets to me. I mean…did he suffer or what?' Maybe he's still alive but I can tell with everyone's face when I say to them he's missing that they all think he's dead. How is your other son?'

'It hit him hard when he lost his brother but he's still there and fighting for his country. It's a terrible war.' Dr. Harding's eyes filled with tears and I could see he was battling to hold them back.

'I'm living in hope anyway,' I said, 'at least for a while. You've got to do, haven't you?'

Before I left, the Harding's thanked me for going. Talking to them helped me too as we all shared the same type of grief.

A few weeks later I saw Mrs. Murray in the street.

'By the way Ruth, I think I have something of yours. I was sat in the easy chair, took some change out of my purse for the window cleaner and dropped it. I saw it go down the side of the chair so pushed my hand down to find it and guess what I did find?' I shook my head. 'I found a gold locket.' My heart skipped a beat. Could it be mine? Mrs. Murray looked at her and smiled. 'I opened it and found your photograph in it with what I gather is your young man.'

'Ooh Mrs. Murray! I thought I'd lost it forever?' I felt my body tingle all over with relief.

'Well you haven't, I've got it.'

'When can I call round for it please?'

'Any time love, it'll be waiting for you.' I dropped the basket I was carrying and hugged Mrs. Murray. 'Well, I didn't expect thanks like that,' she said before continuing on her way and I felt like skipping down the street. I called on her that evening and Mrs. Murray went to the sideboard, opened a drawer and held up the locket.

'I think the fastener needs renewing,' Mrs. Murray showed me how it had been strained and didn't close properly before I burst into tears of relief.

'You'll never know how grateful I am. He's missing you know.'

'I'm so sorry. I know the heartache you're going though. Keep your chin up lass, you never know, he might come home like mine did.'

'Did you get a letter saying he was missing?'

'I did, but I never believed it. I knew in here,' she pointed to her left beast, 'I just knew.'

'Mrs. Murray, you're a life saver. You've given me fresh hope.'

When I went upstairs on my return home, I lay on the bed and opening the locket looked at Billy's photograph. It was the only photograph I had. 'Poor, poor Billy. Where are you my love? Are you alive…or dead? In my heart I felt that he had to be alive as I couldn't see my life without him somehow.

'If only pictures could talk. Oh Billy, I love you so much.'

I held the locket close to my heart for a few minutes as I promised Billy I would. The letters were taken from their Angel box and read all over again before I carefully replaced them. I read the poem and it seemed to take on a different meaning. The poem's message was there—No one could keep us apart because we had an invisible cord to hold us together. He was right. We did have an invisible cord. He can't be dead. The first chance I had, I took the locket to the jewellers to have a new fastener put on it, vowing to myself that I would check the locket on a regular basis in the future as it couldn't, mustn't happen again, not ever. Finding my locket was the best Christmas present I could have. In the evening I went upstairs, lay on my bed and took out Billy's letters again, clutching my locket to my heart as I read them.

Christmas wasn't the same as usual. With the rationing and limited food plus the fact that I had lost Billy didn't make me want to celebrate.

'Come on Ruth you're still alive.' Auntie Lizzie tried to snap me out of my depression but I thought I'd rather be with Billy wherever he was, I just didn't care.

Mary began to show an interest in sewing and for a long time, since she was small, hats had an appeal for her. Helping Auntie Lizzie in whatever way she could with her work, she also attempted to make hats. Auntie Lizzie encouraged her as they sang war songs together. 'Keep the home fires burning,' they sang mostly as it seemed to fit in so well with what was happening, and I would join in sometimes.

I would be in conversation with some of the wounded men who told me tales of the trenches. As Billy never wrote about anything too drastic, I knew there was much to say but knowing Billy, he wouldn't have wanted to upset me.

They would tell me of the horrors they encountered, Lice, filthy clothing, frogs and trench fever. My thoughts often turned to Billy and I wondered what happened and what he'd endured.

I kept my job as a fettler and working conditions were improving all the time. Women were getting a voice and some of the men admitted that without their help the war would go on much longer. Sometimes I helped with first aid by teaching the children.

Visits became less frequent at Billy's parents as my spare time became sparse, then I bumped into Alfred one evening on my way home from first aid. It felt good to see him again and we stopped and chatted.

'How's Sam? I haven't seen Doris to ask her.'

'As far as I know, he's okay. He has some horror stories to tell about the things he sees.'

'I've been hearing about them too.'

'Everyone's talking about it. I feel such a hypocrite at times. I can't go because of my dad's business. I wish I could, if only to show the neighbours who ridicule me for not going to war, but I'm forced to ignore them.'

'It's just one of those things. Think yourself lucky really. My Billy is missing, presumed dead.'

Alfred looked at me and gently held my arm. His understanding made me feel like crying, and the tears filled my eyes.

'Don't Alfred. I'm worried sick and your sympathy isn't making me feel brave.'

In my heart of hearts, I wouldn't accept Billy was gone but at the same time I knew that one day I may have to. 'I'm sorry, I must go home now but it's been lovely seeing you again.'

'May I see you home?' he asked.

I agreed even though I still clung to the fact that it was Billy I wanted. Time was passing by since he went missing and I was lonely, but still I lived in hope that he would come home.

Alfred and I walked in silence for a while, but soon our conversation was as if we'd never been apart. He is an interesting man.

'It must be getting late. I'd better get home. Auntie Lizzie will be worrying.'

'Fatty Arbuckle is on at the Pavilion. I wondered if you would consider allowing me to take you on Saturday,' Alfred asked.

'What about Alice?' I asked. 'Aren't you still going out with her?'

'I tried to see other girls and yes, I did see Alice for a while but I was spoiled by one girl and I couldn't get over her so everyone else paled in comparison.'

'Alfred, Alice is a lovely girl.'

'I agree, she is, but I just couldn't…you know?' He sounded embarrassed so I changed the subject.

'I would love to go to the pictures with you on Saturday Alfred.'

As I entered the house, Lizzie stood there with a quizzical look on her face.

'Who was that you were speaking to?'

'It's a young man I've known for a while,' I answered.

'He looks very nice.'

'He is Aunty Lizzie, he is nice but he's not Billy.'

Before having my supper, I went upstairs and took out Billy's letters yet again. Lying on the bed I read the last one I'd received.

'Where are you Billy? I miss you so much. Do I go out with Alfred or do I wait and see if you come home?' After a while I put the letters carefully away again and went downstairs.

I met Alfred outside the picture house.

'Am I in time for the picture or has it already started.' I asked.

'No, it's not started and yes, you are on time.' He paid and took me inside.

We sat near the back and he held my hand most of the time. As he walked me home we discussed our dreams for the future.

'One day I'd like to get married and have children. I love children and the more the merrier as long as my wife would agree,' Alfred told me as he walked me home. 'I've always envied the large families.'

'You surprise me as you come from a small family,' I replied.

'I think my mam had trouble…you know…woman trouble…I think anyway, but it was never discussed with me. What about you Ruth, do you want children?'

'I love children and I hope to have some one day but you never know, do you? Look at your mam. Maybe she thought the same.'

'You're right of course. Let's hope we both get what we want one day.' He looked down at me and smiled as he squeezed my hand.

I didn't feel about children now as I did when I was with Billy but that was because I wanted Billy's children. It wasn't mentioned again between Alfred and I and when Alfred came to leave me at my door, he asked me if he could see me again.

'Would you like to go for a walk this Sunday? We could go to Stamford Park and I'll take you on the boating lake.'

'Yes Alfred, I think I'd like that.' At least I could reminisce about the past, I thought.

We saw each other occasionally but as the weeks passed it became more often and eventually we became a couple. Alfred took me to the music hall in Ashton and we would join in with the recruitment songs even though Alfred felt rather guilty.

Quite often I would slip into the bedroom at home and open the angel box to read Billy's letters while I looked at his photograph or clutched the locket I still wore. I must have read the poem so many times the paper began to look a little tatty. My heart still breaking over his loss, I would lie on the bed and go over and over the memories I kept in my heart. Why did he have to die? Why did he have to go and join the army? Then I would think about his mother and father and feel guilty enough to go and see them but I never mentioned Alfred.

One evening, while I queued for vegetables in the grocers a few doors away from home, I overheard two women talking. At first, I didn't take much notice of them, one of the women lived around the corner and she had her friend with her whom I gathered was from Ashton. They were deep in conversation and I didn't like to eavesdrop.

'Oh yes, my Clem is wounded all right. He's at the Mechanic's institute on the East Parade.'

'Will he be all right though?' The second woman answered.

'Yes! I tell you who he's with, that Billy Masters.'

My ears picked up Billy's name right away. I couldn't believe it but I also couldn't move with the shock.

'Can you remember them when they were kids? When you visited me they were always playing in the street. Got up to no good. Little scallywags they were. Eeeh! They were little devils, weren't they? I've chased them down the street a few times. Mind you, I couldn't do it now.' They both chortled.

'And what's Billy doing there?'

'He's been shot in the leg.'

I screamed, dropped my basket and fainted. When I recovered, I was sat on a chair with a crowd around me and someone was pushing a piece of cotton wool soaked in ammonia to my nose. Mrs. Watson, the grocer's wife, asked me what I wanted and proceeded to collect it together. As she gave it to me she whispered, 'I've put you three apples in your basket, don't let the others see them because they're on me.' I paid for the items then a man entered the shop and walked towards me.

'Are you all right love?'

I realised it was Uncle George and nodded.

'Do you know this young lady?' Mrs. Watson asked.

'She's my niece.' Uncle George looked at me expecting me to say something but I didn't feel like squabbling about it.

'She might appreciate you walking home with her, it's just up the street but she's just fainted.'

'I think I can do that.' George picked up my basket and helped me to my feet.

'Come on love, let's get you home.'

As soon as we got outside Uncle George asked. 'Are you pregnant?'

'No I am not.' I felt like saying more but because he was helping me, I didn't.

'Last time I saw you, you had a woman on your arm. Are you married now Uncle George?'

Uncle George laughed. 'Me! Nah! not me. Why have one when you can have many?'

I had sometimes seen him around with a woman on his arm and once he called to see me but my Aunt and Uncle made him very unwelcome so he didn't call again. I wondered why my mother hadn't liked him but I shared the same feelings really. He was fond of women, I knew that, and he was much younger than my step-father.

Uncle George made an effort to go inside the house with me but I turned to him to take my basket.

'Thanks a lot. I'm okay now.'

Uncle George passed me my shopping. 'Do I get a kiss for helping you?'

'I don't think that's advisable knowing how sickly I feel.' I thought that would put him off.

Uncle George walked away smiling.

'Auntie Lizzie, Auntie Lizzie,' I called excitedly when I went through the door. 'Guess what? Billy's alive…he's alive.'

'How do you know? Who told you?'

'I've just overheard someone say that he's at the Mechanics in Ashton. I'm going.'

When Auntie Lizzie unpacked the groceries, she found one of the apples missing. Auntie Lizzie cursed Uncle George when I told her he had brought me home.

'What can you expect from your Dad's brother? He's rotten! Fancy him taking advantage of you when you needed help like that.' I was shocked at her tone of voice as I never heard my aunt speak like that about anyone before. What was it that made some women seek him out and others hate him so much? As I didn't feel in the mood for a conversation I excused myself to get ready to go and see Billy. Going into my bedroom I began to search through my clothes. I had to find something that I knew Billy would like. There weren't many clothes to choose from so I soon had an outfit ready and waiting, but first I must do my hair and put on a little colour for my cheeks because I looked too pale. As much as I wanted to look my best for Billy, I couldn't wait to see him, so I rushed it. After checking myself in the mirror I was ready.

Auntie Lizzie called me for my tea but I declined and appeared in my coat again.

'I have to go to the Mechanics Auntie. Billy's alive, I can't believe it...and he's injured.' I didn't look forward to seeing Billy hurt but seeing him in any state would be wonderful.

'Get some food inside you first dear; you don't look a bit well.' I shook my head and Auntie Lizzie reached for one of the two apples. 'Here take this and eat it on the way.'

I put my arms around my Auntie and hugged her. 'Have I ever told you how much I love you and Uncle Jim?'

'I know, I know. Go on with you. Don't forget to eat your apple; you can eat it while you're walking.'

'Okay.' I pushed the apple into my pocket and after telling Mary where I was going and why, I went out into the street. My fingers rolled the apple around inside my coat. I would save it for Billy; he would need building up. Heaven only knows what state I would find him in.

When I finally reached the Mechanics' Institute, I wandered through the door and looked around. There were many wounded soldiers, some of them on makeshift beds and some on the floor, some wounds you could see and some you couldn't. It also smelled of sweat mixed up with disinfectant and cigarette smoke. Finding him was difficult but then I saw him, he was sat on a mattress on the wooden floor. As I went closer I could see he wore shorts, the top of his leg was bandaged and the blood had soaked through.

'Billy,' I shouted or was it a scream? My feet didn't seem to touch the floor as I weaved through the wounded soldiers to throw myself at his side. Tears streaming down my cheeks I placed my hands on each side of his face and kissed his forehead, nose, cheeks and finally his lips.

'Poor, poor Billy.' I uttered almost under my breath.

'How did you know I was here?' His voice was almost a whisper.

'I overheard it mentioned in a conversation between two women, but why didn't *you* let me know?'

'I had my reasons.' He turned away and when I put my hand on his face to bring him to face me he had tears in his eyes.

'Look Billy, I'm still wearing the locket. I've never taken it off; it's been there all the time.' It was just a little fib of no consequence. I couldn't understand why he was so quiet. 'What's the matter Billy, don't you love me anymore?'

I could see the muscles in his jaw move as if he was clenching his teeth. 'I just think you'd be better without me that's all.' He turned to the young soldier next to him and I recognised him as Billy's friend.

'Have you got a cig Clem?' Billy asked, and then turned his back to me while the soldier fumbled in his pocket. Clem gave him a cigarette and put one in his own mouth.

'Do you smoke?' Clem asked. I shook my head.

'Have you got a light as well?' Billy asked, 'as it's no good without one.' Clem reached inside his pocket and brought out a lighter which he flicked open and lit Billy's cigarette then his own. Billy puffed at it and I watched as the smoke he blew out disappeared.

I became agitated and my voice rose with worry. 'What do you mean Billy, why would I be better without you?'

'I'm no good for you anymore, leave me be.'

'Billy, what are you talking about? What's the matter, are you going to tell me or not?'

Clem next to him leaned over. 'Go on lad, tell her the truth, can't you see she loves you?'

Billy turned to me and he still had tears in his eyes. He wiped them away on the sleeve of his jacket. 'Do you…do you *really* love me?'

'You know I do.'

'Enough? I wonder…'

I laughed nervously. 'What are you talking about, you daft thing?'

'I mean *really* love me,' he pleaded.

'I wouldn't care if you were crippled for life…with no legs, I'd still want you…is that enough?' I laughed nervously again in case it wasn't. He wrapped his arms about me and squeezed me so hard I thought I would stop breathing. 'Oh, Billy, you had me worried then.'

'Tell her…go on.' Again the other soldier urged him on.

'Oh shut up Clem.' Turning to me Billy hung his head and quietly murmured 'I'm finding this very hard because I know how you love children. You're so good with your Mary, I just felt as if I couldn't do it to you.' My face paled.

'What?' I hesitated. 'Y…you…mean you can't have children? But you've only been shot in your leg haven't you?'

All the colour drained from his face. 'You see, it does matter. The bullet passed through my leg and into…' He pulled away his pants a little at the waist and revealed more bandages, then noticed my face. 'I knew it would make a difference and I was right.' He turned away.

Realisation eventually hit me. 'C'mon. As if that matters…well it does really because I won't have any little Billys' running around the place.'

Billy turned back to face me. 'Unfortunately, there'd be no little Ruthies' too.' He looked absolutely miserable. 'If you really mind, say so now. I'll understand.'

'Come 'ere.' I put my arms round his neck and we held each other for a while. My mind worked overtime. Perhaps the doctors were wrong and he would heal enough to give me children. They're not always right. It can't be true. Then he kissed me and that made me feel much better.

'Will you marry me Ruth, even though I'm only half the man I was?'

'Yes Billy Masters! I will. And to me you'll always be a complete man—and you're my man!'

Clem next to him cheered.

'I always wanted you to marry me Ruth but first of all I'd like you to give it a lot of thought…I mean, really think.' His eyes looked into mine and I knew if there was a time for a change of heart it was now. Biting my bottom lip I paused for a few tense seconds.

'Try and stop me soldier.'

Clem cheered again. 'Hey everybody, they're getting married.'

One of the other soldiers across the room shouted back, 'Not another one? in a bored voice.

'No, not another one,' echoed Billy, 'ours will be the only one…a special one.' He kissed me lovingly, longingly. 'Be very sure Ruth, I won't hold you to this decision so you can still change your mind.'

I remembered the apple. 'Here Billy, have this, you'll need it.' I realised how hungry and light headed I felt. 'I'd better go home now. I'll see you tomorrow.' Bending over I kissed him again. 'Goodnight my love, my future husband.' We waved until I disappeared through the door. As I ran down the steps I bumped into my old friend.

'Hiya Doris, I haven't seen you for ages, what have you been doing with yourself? Are you still going with Sam?'

'I've been in France for a while but came home with some of the wounded and as for Sam…well…it's something we can maybe continue when this terrible war is over. We do try to keep in touch.'

'How long were you in France?' Going to France was something I intended to do if I could, but I couldn't go now.

'Too long, it was terrible Ruth. Both Alice and I applied. I've never seen her since, I think she must have had a different posting.'

'I didn't realise.' I had wondered where they were as I hadn't seen them for a while.

'You should have been there Ruth or maybe not. At least you won't have nightmares for the rest of your life.'

'Was it that bad?'

'You wouldn't believe it. When I arrived in France I had a shock when I saw the conditions.'

Thinking about Billy, I asked 'Was it really bad?'

Doris looked pale and drawn. 'Bad! It was terrible. We had to work with the basics. Wounded men lying on the ground waiting for surgery or else they'd be in dirty beds full of lice, you have no idea. They're even coming home full of lice now and they're stinking. Ambulances were always coming and going through the noise of shelling.

'It sounds as if you've really been through it Doris.'

'You had to be there Ruth to understand just how bad it was. I tried to help the ones who could hardly walk to a suitable place to lie down and the smell of their wounds would make me retch.'

'Oh!' Ruth's thoughts turned to what Billy must have gone through. 'It must have been absolutely awful!'

'It was. I doused them with Lysol.' Pausing a moment to pull her face. 'I had to use it whenever necessary and that was too often. Sometimes they were full of maggots. Uggh! I had to be brutal. I could see one with lice running around in the wound and that was awful.'

'Oh Doris!' I cringed.

'Why is there a war Ruth? Why do people take great pleasure in killing and maiming others? Would we really do such things to each other if we could see the results?'

'I'm so sorry.'

'I suppose I shouldn't have gone but at the time I thought why not! I'm a hard worker and I love the work, so why not try! I never in my wildest nightmares realised what I was in for.'

'Oh Doris,' I sympathised.

'Amputations were the worst! Uggh, they were awful. Legs really got through to me. I imagined those men in the future. The thought of him never walking again and playing football and cricket like ordinary men; or even playing with his future children. It just isn't fair!' They didn't start the war but they were the ones to suffer for the rest of their lives.'

Doris stopped to retrieve a handkerchief from her pocket and wipe the tears from her face as I went over in my mind what I would have done had I seen Billy like that. Doris didn't notice my faraway look and would have carried on anyway.

'Hands were upsetting too. I wrote countless letters for them and struggled to explain to their loved ones their injuries with the least distress. How would they manage in the future? Eventually, I learned to shut these thoughts from my mind and try to get on with my work. When they were dying, some of them would ask to hold my hand and that's something I shall never forget.

Watching them take their last breath was very distressing but at the same time I felt privileged too as I was the chosen one for them to share the last minutes of their life...better me than the enemy.'

I watched the tears rolling down my friend's face again as she spoke and wiped them away constantly. I didn't mention Billy proposing to me, it wasn't the right time...and then there was Alfred, poor Alfred...I'd forgotten him. Heck!

Chapter 12

I met Alfred on our arranged date but I refused to go to the pictures with him as we planned. We went for a walk and found a quiet place to sit while I told him about Billy and why I had to finish with him. He became upset and I could see the unshed tears in his eyes.

'I just feel like this keeps happening. You know I love you but I always knew I came second to Billy.'

'It's hard for me too you know Alfred. I have become very fond of you but I can't turn my back on Billy now.'

'You mean because he's wounded?'

'Well yes…but Alfred…I've always loved him…always will.' I sought his hand and held it. 'Please be happy for me.'

'That goes without saying but you know if anything goes wrong, I'll always be there waiting. You know that don't you?'

'Don't do this Alfred. You're a lovely man so find someone else to love you as you deserve to be loved.'

'I don't think that will happen.'

'But what about the children you want? You'll have to find someone if you want children.'

'Don't they say if you've never had something then you won't miss it?'

'Now you're making me feel awful.'

'There's no need to. Just be happy.'

'What time is it? I'm in a bit of a hurry.'

Alfred showed me the time on his watch, and then held me close for the last time.

'Don't forget what I said, I'll always be waiting.'

I walked away, turned and waved to him then didn't dare turn my head again because I knew I'd break down and cry.

§§§§§§

I went to see Billy whenever I could and he began to improve with his health. He finally went home. His Mother fussed over him until he was on his feet again. He had a permanent limp and needed a walking stick but that didn't matter to me.

Food was in short supply but only the poor suffered as the rich could afford to pay the 'Black Market' prices, so rationing began to help food be shared out more fairly. Everyone was issued with ration cards, I believe even the King and Queen had them but I couldn't see them going short of anything. The rations were enough for the family but I often wondered how the rich went on as it must have been a greater hardship for them. All the same, I supposed they had some way of avoiding doing without. When you had the money you appeared to do okay. By April, our rations were just enough to feed us. We had to register at one shop and only use that one for our rations. The government controlled many other goods too. Most people accepted it even though we did not like the idea but we had no choice.

Rationing also solved the problems of rising prices and food queues. Even more surprising, the health of the majority of people actually improved as a result of it! The poor got a share of better food than they could have afforded before and the well off ate less of the food that was bad for them.

A flu epidemic began and over a short time there were many people who caught it and many who died. Uncle Jim caught the flu and Auntie Lizzie insisted that we kept away from him, and then we wouldn't catch it. Before long, Auntie Lizzie came down with it and then I needed to take over the nursing of them both, plus looking after Mary. I told Billy to keep away until things returned to normal. I battled with changing pinafores for nursing and washing my hands every time I left my Auntie and Uncle as I tried to keep the germs at bay to protect Mary. I missed Billy so much and hoped they would both feel better soon for all our sakes.

I remembered a lot of things that Grandma Tyson taught me and one good thing was the invalid recipes. When my Auntie and Uncle wouldn't or couldn't eat what we were having then I would make them some beef tea or chicken custard to keep their strength up. I encouraged them to drink milk and if they could eat a boiled egg I would feel more satisfied. The 'flu affected many neighbours too and it was a long time before Uncle Jim felt better and longer still before he went back to work. At least we were thankful we had come through it, as there were thousands who didn't.

All the wounded soldiers were given the freedom of the town and many of their uniforms, light blue flannel with white shirt and red tie, or 'wounded blue' as they were called by the locals, were seen around. They were given privileges for a while and would take small jobs when they could. Billy looked very handsome in his uniform. There were parties galore for the wounded men but meanwhile the war still went on.

The push towards the German border began on October seventeenth, nineteen eighteen. French, American armies and the British advanced. Turkey signed an armistice at the end of October, Austria-Hungary followed on November the third.

Germany crumbled from within. The sailors of the High Seas Fleet mutinied on October twenty ninth. November the ninth, the Kaiser abdicated; he slipped into the Netherlands and exile. At five in the morning on November the eleventh, an armistice was signed in a railroad car parked in a French forest near the front lines.

The terms of the agreement called for the cessation of fighting along the entire Western Front beginning at precisely eleven that morning. After over four years of bloody conflict, the Great War was at an end.

At the front there was no celebration.

The firing continued after eleven o'clock that day and there were men who fell unnecessarily. The soldiers couldn't believe it was over and expected more orders to start firing again.

The world celebrated. There was dancing in the streets and the drinking of champagne if you had it, or any other alcoholic drink if you didn't. There were street parties and lots and lots of laughter which had been suppressed for too long.

Some of the soldiers in the trenches suffered a total nervous collapse. Some hoped they would return home to their loved ones. Some thought of the temporary little crosses that marked the graves of their comrades. Some fell asleep, exhausted. All were bewildered.

The armistice was signed and came into effect at 11:00 a.m. on November 11, 1918.

Billy eventually told me what happened when he went missing after I'd asked him many times. At first he said he couldn't go through it all again as the memories were too painful but at last he allowed it all to come tumbling out.

'There was a terrible explosion from a shell that landed nearby and when I awoke I found myself alone and almost buried in soil. The enemy came and helped me out. I must have looked a sight…half dead with my clothes in tatters and my head, having lost my helmet, full of dried blood and mucky. I don't remember how I got to the dressing station, didn't really care at the time. I did become aware that I was sleeping next to the men I was fighting not long before though.'

'Someone woke me up who could speak English and told me from now on my duties were to carry their wounded up the line. The things I saw made my stomach turn over. Men with legs blown away...allsorts! Most of the prisoners, including me, and lots of the enemy had dysentery. It made me realise how wicked a war really is. It didn't seem right that I had to load shells on their lorries that were taking them to their soldiers for them to kill *our* men, but I didn't have a choice.

'I kept trying to figure out how to escape and once or twice I almost did but there was always something or someone who stopped my efforts. Our stretchers were long poles with a piece of material tied by the four corners to them. Carrying the wounded back to the dressing station, we were under fire from our own men all the time...if they only knew. I prayed for help for a way to escape and finally my chance came...and that's how I got shot, but I was determined it wouldn't stop me so I crawled to safety.

'We were allowed one bath a month while we were prisoners and our clothes were fumigated, it felt good at the time but it wasn't long before the insects came back, we were alive with them. Our quarters were in old barrack rooms and they were unbelievable. We had very little food and I was so hungry that I almost swapped my boots for something to eat. The bread and jam they gave us didn't even taste like bread and jam but that was because it wasn't. Everything wasn't real. Most were substituted with something else. I had nightmares at times and lost sleep. At night before I went to sleep I tried to concentrate on you to keep the nightmares away.'

'Oh Billy,' I held his hand and kissed his fingers.

It was after Christmas that Billy asked Auntie Lizzie and Uncle Jim for my hand in marriage and they agreed. A few months later we were married. That day was the day of the Black Knight Pageant and we stood and watched it after the wedding with the family. It was a kind of celebration, not only of the black knight but the war being over and our marriage too. There were people dressed in different costumes from the olden days, dancing girls and children (they were always lovely to watch) and then the knight on a Black horse who was booed as he rode past on his horse.

'Who is the Black Knight?' asked Mary.

Auntie Lizzie replied, 'He was an evil, rich knight, a favourite of King Richard the third, who would ride to Ashton every Easter Monday murdering people who allowed the corn marigolds to grow in his fields. He murdered lots of people before he was finally shot.'

Mary thought about that for a while then asked, 'Who shot him and what did they shoot him with?

Aunty Lizzie tut-tutted. 'This child asks the most awkward questions at times. I don't know Mary. I don't know who shot him or what with but somebody killed him all those years ago and we've celebrated it ever since.' After the last of the pageant passed we went home to have a special tea, joined by Auntie Lizzie, Uncle Jim, Mary and Billy's parents.

We started our married life living with Auntie Lizzie and Uncle Jim. We were allowed to use my bedroom and the run of the house. As me and Billy didn't like to put too much pressure on them, we looked around for a rented house of our own but could never find one we could afford.

Billy had terrible nightmares. I would be wakened by his screams and sometimes he would thrash out. I received a few bruises for a while and hoped people believed me when I told them they were through his nightmares.

After the war the mills were booming and I worked hard trying to put a little away towards our own home. Billy did his best to find work but found it difficult so he started cutting hair for a little extra money.

Mary left school and instead of going in the mill with me, she joined Auntie Lizzie in the sewing room as she appeared to have a talent for making clothes. One evening Auntie Lizzie came in from shopping all flushed and excited.

'Ruth, get yourself to see Ernie Walker, he's got a house for rent on the bottom of Railway Street. It's that one that's empty just round the corner. You'll be near us if you get it and the rent isn't high.'

'Right, I'll go straight away.'

I untied my apron and hung it on the back of the door. Lizzie watched me as I half ran up the street. A while later I returned, with a big smile on my face, and holding the key to the house round the corner.

'I've got it,' I dangled the key from a string on my finger. Auntie Lizzie hugged me and we danced around the kitchen. Mary joined us followed by Uncle Jim. They were not sure what it was all about at first but they gathered that if it was something to dance about, it must be good.

When Billy arrived home, after searching all day for a job, we all went to view the house. It was filthy; obviously had Blackjacks as Lizzie called them, as we found a few dead ones. I called them beetles but they were big, whatever their name happened to be. We did have them in our own house as they would come up through the cracks in the slate floors but not as many as we saw in the one we viewed. The house showed promise though. It had a large front room and a big kitchen with a cold tap over the usual brown slop stone sink, two bedrooms upstairs and a shared toilet in the big back at the rear of the terraced houses plus the yard was a nice size. Auntie Lizzie and Uncle Jim promised to help them to clean it. When the others left, me and Billy stood in the middle of the front room and looked around.

'Our first home.' My eyes filled with tears.

'Are you still sure you want me?' Billy held me close.

'I've never been so sure of anything in my life. Anyway, I married you didn't I? so I can't do anything about that now can I?' I pushed my hands through his hair and laughed as it stood on end. I kissed the tip of his nose and whispered. 'What do you think about having Mary with us?'

He held me at arms length. 'I think it's a brilliant idea. I know how much she means to you.'

'It's whether my Auntie and Uncle will agree.'

'I'm sure they will.' He winked at me knowing they wouldn't refuse me anything.

After locking up *our* house, Billy and I held hands as we made our way back home. As soon as we arrived we sought out Auntie Lizzie and Uncle Jim.

'What do you think about Mary coming to live with us? I asked.

'I thought she might,' answered Auntie Lizzie, 'at least until you have children.'

Me and Billy silently looked at each other.

'And I think she'd like that too,' Uncle Jim added.

I found Mary in the bedroom and put my plan forward.

'What do you think of the house?' I asked.

'I'm very happy for you. It must be a lovely feeling.' Mary paused for a while then spoke almost to herself, 'I'll miss you both.'

I laughed. 'Well, you don't have to because we wondered if you would like to move in with us.'

Mary was so excited she could hardly speak but finally she croaked, 'I can't believe it.'

Me and Mary went downstairs and sat at the table with our heads together and discussed our new home, what furniture we would need, and even adding ornaments in our discussion, while Billy sat and watched us. We were so excited. Billy tried to add things too but gave up after a while as our excitement took over.

'Can I have the front bedroom? It would be great for me to have that sewing machine in there that Auntie Lizzie and Uncle Jim bought me, and then I'll have the room for my dressmaking.'

'No Mary, that's for Billy and me.'

'But I…'

'Mary…no. You can't have everything.'

Mary could see that I meant it so didn't pursue it.

Before she had a chance to move in, a letter arrived for her. Mary read it and became quite excited. Dancing round the room she sang 'I'm going to live with Auntie Hilda, Auntie Hilda's is where I want to be and she wants me…' to a made up tune of her own.

When she calmed down, Auntie Lizzie sat and talked to her about it, explaining that it would be a different life to what she knew, as London was a busy place.

'Since she lost her husband, Uncle Arthur, in the Titanic, Aunty Hilda is very lonely so I know that she will look after you, but you must be aware that there were many thieves and beggars that you would need to look out for.'

Mary promised she would remember to be aware and be very careful. The following day Auntie Lizzie received a letter from Auntie Hilda explaining that Mary would have the best of tutors who would teach her everything she would need to know about sewing.

We eventually waved Mary off after she promised she would write and we watched her as she disappeared down the street and round the corner. Somehow, the house seemed empty without her.

Our house did need a lot of cleaning. Auntie Lizzie and I would go at every opportunity and scrub it everywhere. My Auntie made curtains and Billy got busy making a pegged rug. I bought a few things, borrowed a few things and begged the rest, concentrating on essentials like a bed, table and a couple of dining chairs plus kettle, pans and a few bits of crockery and cutlery. Most of the things Auntie Lizzie gave to us and some were given by Billy's parents, friends and neighbours who had no more use for them. We acquired furniture wherever we could and didn't refuse anything. Orange boxes made shelves and bedside tables. Me and Billy eventually moved into our house after we were satisfied it was clean enough.

We couldn't believe our luck, our own home. We settled in and Billy made and repaired what he could. One day I came home from work and there was a jam jar full of roses in the middle of the table.

'Where have they come from,' I asked.

'I cut a man's hair and he had no money to give me so I settled for these roses from his garden.'

'Oh Billy, they're beautiful.' They were a deep red and I cut one of the blooms and pushed it into the buttonhole in Billy's jacket. He looked down at the flower and kissed me on the cheek.

After such a boom in the cotton industry the crash came as a shock. Some said it wouldn't last long but there was too much going on abroad for things to go back to normal and so jobs were few. Those who thought they were safe found themselves on the dole and this didn't last for long. People stood at the factory gates and waited for someone to appear and pick out certain ones to work. I found myself at the gates far too many times but I was one of the lucky ones that were quite often chosen.

There were many limbless service men and many who'd deserted. They found it difficult to find a job and Billy still found it difficult. Obviously the job situation was bad enough for the fit as there were not enough jobs to go around. Uncle Jim still worked on the trams. Billy tried hard but I knew his leg bothered him so a job standing all day was definitely out. He began to mend shoes to bring in a little bit more. When he was in the army, he learned to cut the men's hair so with that and mending shoes, although he didn't earn much, we managed with my wages. At least he could take his time with his jobs and if his leg bothered him he could sit down.

The years that followed were hard for most people. Men were throwing themselves in the canal when things became really tough. I changed my job many times, working in whichever mill when I heard they needed winders. Sometimes I would use a short cut walking over the canal to find work. On the odd occasion I would see a body floating on the top while someone was battling to fish it out. Things were bad.

Chapter 13

Auntie Lizzie would get letters from Aunty Hilda to say how much Mary was learning. Any special holiday weekend Mary would come home for a few days and she blossomed into an attractive young woman with her dark curly hair that was just like her Dad's. Mary showed how adept she had become with a needle too. Often, she would see a dress in a shop window, buy the nearest match of material, and make an identical dress in no time at all.

Uncle Jim became ill and had to stay off work and Mary came home to help the family.

'I couldn't stay with Auntie Hilda while my Uncle is poorly, I wouldn't be able to concentrate,' she said as she hugged both Auntie Lizzie and then me.

Auntie Lizzie tried to get more orders to keep food on our table. Times were hard but Auntie Lizzie worked when she could while looking after Uncle Jim, and Mary took over most of the sewing. There were many poor people and they would ask them to do much needed repairs to their existing clothes. I took in anything, darning socks, patching and mending torn clothes. Between us we made a small income which put food on the table and I did my best to help with the repairs whenever I could. Sometimes we did mending for nothing if there was the usual sob story. One Sunday morning, Auntie Lizzie got up, made Uncle Jim's breakfast and took it up to him in bed. She said his forehead felt very hot so she asked me to call the doctor.

'I don't know,' Auntie Lizzie said, 'he managed to get through that flu epidemic a while ago but he's looking really ill now, I wonder if it's weakened him.'

'Will you be able to give him something to clear it up Doctor Harding?' Auntie Lizzie asked when the doctor called.

'I can give you something but he'll need a lot of care. I'm afraid he's really ill Lizzie and you'll need to work hard to pull him through this time.'

Auntie Lizzie sobbed for a long time after that news, and although I attempted to console her, I couldn't.

A few days later, I was already working hard with the latest mending when I heard my Aunt scream. I dropped the socks I were darning and ran upstairs. Auntie stood as white as a sheet.

'What's the matter?' I asked as I placed my arm around Lizzie's shoulders.

Auntie Lizzie's eyes were glazed and she stood shaking. I looked at Uncle Jim who lay with his eyes half open. Without much ado I went for the doctor while Mary looked after Auntie Lizzie. Dr. Harding came as soon as he could and I took him upstairs where he examined Uncle Jim. As the doctor packed his bag to go he looked at me.

'Keep your eye on Lizzie Ruth, she's had a shock. Your Aunt thought he'd gone.' Pulling her on one side he whispered, 'I don't think he has long.'

I nodded and after going back downstairs to see the doctor out who promised to call again later, I walked over to my Aunt. 'C'mon Auntie Lizzie, let's have a nice cup of tea. Uncle Jim is okay but he'll need your strength.'

Auntie Lizzie sobbed. 'I know Doctor Harding thinks Jim won't make it …but he's got to. I can't live without him.'

'He doesn't know how strong he is but we do and we're not giving up on him. We'll look after him between us. We'll sit up all night if we have to.'

I went back into the kitchen and filled a bowl with cold water, picked up a cloth and took it upstairs. Uncle Jim looked pale as he lay in bed between the white sheets. I looked around the room. It must have been really hard for my Aunt and Uncle when they took us in after the fire. Not only did they have so much extra work, but they needed extra food and clothing too. As they already had Grandma to keep, it must have been difficult, but they never complained. I supposed it helped when Grandma began to draw a pension. At least she had spending money for any little luxuries she wanted to buy. Not that she did, she was always treating us with any money she had.

The room was clean and tidy but very shabby. The floorboards needed repair and polishing and the pegged rug at the side of the bed looked a little sorry for itself. Maybe one day I would make another rug for my Auntie. Memories returned of when I helped my Grandma to make the one downstairs. My job was to cut up any old clothes that were beyond repair into strips, and then my Grandma would peg them into the sacking. When Grandma produced a new peg she bought for me, I was over the moon. I smiled at the memory and felt so grateful for the love we had all been given. Bending over, I kissed my Uncle Jim. He was too hot so I dampened the cloth and wiped his face. I opened a drawer and took out spare sheets which Auntie

Lizzie used for the spare bed we had placed in the bedroom close to Uncle Jim. Making it as comfortable as I could I again dampened the cloth and wiped my Uncles' face. Eventually I took the bowl downstairs again and changed the water. After Auntie Lizzie drank her tea, I encouraged her to go and get in the spare bed that I had just made up for her while I tended Uncle Jim.

Billy came to help us and took his turn at sitting up to give us a rest.

We kept this up day and night, cooling him and Auntie Lizzie would give him a bed bath to help things along. He was delirious for a while but finally, his temperature started to come down.

It was Lizzie that went upstairs with Jim's breakfast and found him. He must have died suddenly after I left the spare bed. I called Dr. Harding.

When the doctor came, Auntie Lizzie was in bed, after much persuasion from me, and she got up as soon as she heard the doctor's voice. I took him upstairs. We went into the bedroom where my Uncle Jim lay.

'I think his heart gave out.' Dr. Harding said. 'He had a bad time.'

'I know, but we did try our best.'

'You know he was lucky to last as long as this. You must have all taken good care of him.'

'We did. We loved him.'

'Then he was a lucky man.'

The funeral took place the following week and there were many people there who knew him beside the relatives. Peter, Uncle Jim's nephew, and Beth and Percy with baby Joan came and Auntie Hilda also came along with the rest of the surviving family. There were many of the men who worked with Uncle Jim in the church too, as my Uncle Jim regularly went on a Sunday.

'He was very well respected,' one of them told Auntie Lizzie. 'A good man.'

Auntie Hilda didn't stay very long and made Mary promise to return to London to finish her training.

One day Mary went to Ashton for much needed buttons, needles and pins. When she returned she told me that she found herself facing Peter, her cousin, who worked at Kershaw's drapers shop.

'How are you Mary? Peter asked, how nice to see you. I didn't see much of you at the funeral.'

'That's nice,' I said.

Mary continued. 'I told him I stayed with Aunt Hilda in London for a while, and then came home when Uncle Jim was ill. He asked me if I was going back so I told him I'd have problems if I stayed. He said he hoped I'd stay.' Mary blushed as she told me. 'And…' she said, 'he asked me if he could take me to the pictures.'

I was so pleased for her as I know she always liked him right from being a little girl. After that he was never away from our house.

Mary decided she would go back to London after a few weeks and Peter looked very disappointed.

I overheard them talking. 'I'm going to miss you Mary. I don't know why you have to go.'

'I think it's better. I did promise Aunty Hilda I would go and finish my training. It won't be forever, I'll be back before you know it.'

Mary went back to London and was missed by me and Auntie Lizzie. Peter often asked after her too when we called at the shop for sewing materials.

A few months later, an old work friend of mine asked me if I would like to join her and a few friends to a dance the following week. Billy urged me to go.

'It will take you out of yourself. You haven't been the same since your Uncle took ill and it will be a break for you.'

I felt a little unsure, 'But, I don't know Billy.'

'I know you always liked dancing, and *I* can't take you, so you go. I couldn't dance before my war injury so I'm damned sure I can't now.'

When the day came, I put on my favourite dress, a brand new one that was a lovely colour of blue. I'd only tried it on once. Lizzie made me the dress a short time before Uncle Jim became ill and I'd never worn it because I felt that I shouldn't. This was it! Auntie Lizzie wouldn't see it so it wouldn't upset her. It was an ideal opportunity for me to wear it. I checked myself in the mirror and admitted to myself that the dress did fit me well and brought out the blue in my eyes. I kissed Billy before I left and he promised to wait up until I came home. My friend called for me and we walked up the street giggling like two schoolgirls.

At first, I really enjoyed myself. There were many of the girls I worked with from the past there and it was nice to renew acquaintances. Also there were a few men I knew who asked me to dance. After a while I grew tired and joined my friend who sat smoking a cigarette. She offered me one but I refused. After smoking another, she encouraged me to try one. I watched her for a while and after I was shown how she made smoke rings I gave in and tried one. After a coughing fit I gradually became accustomed to it and sat fascinated watching the rings I was blowing into the air. As the evening wore on I developed a headache and a bad taste in my mouth. Whether it was the heat or smoke from the cigarettes or even a combination of both I didn't know. After a while, I told my friend I was going home and after refusing to allow her to spoil her evening by escorting me home, I left to walk home alone.

It was dark, and I pulled the collar of my coat up to protect my neck from the slight wind. My footsteps echoed as I walked and I wondered how long it had been since I walked alone through the streets at night. There weren't many people around until, as I came close to the canal, I saw a couple ahead of me. The young man's arm was around the girl's waist as he guided her towards the tow path. It would be quicker to go that way and I was in a hurry to get home. Feeling I would be safe walking behind them, I turned my footsteps to follow them. It was dark with a little moonlight that flickered along the top of the water and an odd lamp light here and there. A breeze ruffled my hair and I pulled my coat further up my neck to keep it warm. My thoughts turned back to when I played there with my friend Doris. We would lie on our bellies and catch tiddlers from the canal. Sometimes it would be newts. I could see us both now, searching for something to put our latest catch in. Happy days! Or it was until my Auntie Lizzie caught me and then there was hell to pay.

After a while, the couple stopped and started kissing. I felt I had gone too far to turn back, especially as I wasn't feeling very well and couldn't wait to get home so I carried on along the path. There were too few lamps that shone their light but the half moon gave me enough light to see my way. I shivered; it wasn't because of the temperature but…it was quiet, dark and I felt very alone. My footsteps quickened. If I felt better I would have run the rest of the way but I didn't feel well at all and couldn't wait to see Billy and get into bed.

This was a particular dark corner just before the bridge that would take me over the canal and into the giggle gaggle. Even the moon couldn't shine its light here but I didn't have far to go now. I shivered again. The steps behind me were quiet and I heard them too late. I felt a hand over my mouth that stifled my scream and I could feel myself being dragged under the bridge. Fighting with all the strength I could muster I had no chance. It was a strong hand holding my mouth and my breath came in gasps as I fought my attacker. Now he was pushing me back onto the floor and I kicked and scratched but there was no release. The stench of stale beer and sweat filled my nostrils and as he held my wrist in a steel grip I could feel a lump in the middle of his hand. For a moment he eased his grip and I grabbed his hand and scratched and pressed on the lump as hard as I could thinking it was some kind of nasty boil and it would hurt him, but I was wrong.

I could hear a tearing sound as he pulled up my dress and I felt his hand on my leg. I managed to grab him again and tried to force him away from my groin but to no avail. Again I felt the lump on the palm of his hand and pressed hard, hoping it brought him pain and he would release me but there was still no response. He thumped me in the face so it was me who felt the pain, especially when he pushed himself inside me. I couldn't struggle anymore as a wave of sickness overcame me and just before I fully passed out I felt my dress being pulled over my head.

As I began to come round I heard a splash. Opening my eyes I felt cold then realised I was half naked. I felt bruised and sore and went to rub my elbow to ease the pain but found it was grazed and bleeding. My knees were throbbing from the struggle and I could feel the stickiness of the blood clinging to me. I felt around for my clothes. 'Oh, God, please let me find something to wear.' Sobbing uncontrollably I got on my hands and knees, crawling and feeling for my clothes. It was so dark under the bridge. I groped around the dirt and imagined what Billy would say. I felt as if I would die. The splash! Of course! It must have been my shoes. I felt my dress, that was something but it was ripped. I put it on and then fumbled about for something else but there was nothing. Not finding anything to wear, I realised the man must have thrown everything into the canal. Luckily, I wasn't far from home. Trying hard to hold my dress together I walked over the bridge then realised I had blood running down my leg. I dragged myself through the giggle gaggle in my stocking feet. I heard Billy's voice before I reached the street. Peeping round the corner I could see him stood on the doorstep talking to Nellie, my neighbour. Returning to the shadows of the giggle gaggle I waited.

'Oh please go home,' I said silently.

Their voices quietened and I peeped around the corner again. Nellie had disappeared so I hurried to our house where Billy was just going to shut the door. I was so grateful there was no one around.

'Oh-my-God! What on earth happened to you?' Ushering me into the house, he helped me to the chair. His face full of concern he asked, 'What happened?' I clung to him.

'Oh Billy,' I cried. 'I'm bleeding.'

'Who did this?' his fists clenched as he became angrier.

'I don't know Billy, I don't want to know and I know you wouldn't be responsible for your actions if you found out. He must have waited for me on the canal.' I cried until I felt I couldn't cry anymore, I was exhausted.

'Who did it?'

I shouted back. 'I don't know. He ravished me Billy. He *ravished* me. I'm bleeding.'

Billy rolled up the sleeves of his shirt. 'Which way did he go? he asked.

'Billy, he's gone. Don't leave me…I didn't see him…I passed out.'

I staggered into the kitchen and filled a pan with water. I must wash all the filth away. Reaching for the cloth I couldn't wait for the water to heat and I began to wash myself as hard as I could, crying, sobbing and sometimes shouting with pain as I scrubbed at the grazes.

'Billy, please can you get the bath and fill it for me. I need to wash; I'm desperate to wash this away. I can't stand it…please!' Billy's eyes were wide and angry as he tried to control himself so that he could help me. He went into the yard and returned with the tin bath where he began to prepare the hot water. Eventually, he tested it.

His voice clipped, he said 'Get in.' I looked at him.

'I couldn't help it Billy.' Billy shook his head.

'If I ever get hold of that blighter...I'll kill him.'

I got into the bath and sat in there for a long time, scrubbing myself, trying to clean my body. When he offered me a basin for me to wash my hair I accepted it, but his offer to help to wash my back I absolutely refused until finally I asked him for a towel. After rubbing myself dry until Billy thought I must be red raw I finally pulled on my night-gown.

'I'll kill him! I will. Whoever the bugger is.' I hardly ever heard Billy swear in my presence. He was obviously very angry.

'Don't ever tell anyone, will you?' I begged.

'I'd like to know who the devil it was.' His voice became raised. 'What on earth made you walk over the canal? It was a stupid thing to do, you know that! Fancy walking over there in the dark. You were asking for trouble.'

'Billy!' I screamed at him. 'How can you say that?'

Billy cried. 'I'm so sorry I, I didn't mean that...but you know what I mean.'

'Please! Let's not argue about it...I felt ill that's why I came home early...I thought I was safe...because there was a couple...but they stopped...and it was too late to turn back...I...I couldn't help it...' My breath gone, I just sobbed.

Billy sat with his arms around me, hugging me and squeezing me. 'I'm not blaming you, not really love...but I'll murder him if I ever find out who he is...now try to forget it...if you can. It doesn't matter.'

'Oh Billy he hurt me so much.'

'I bet he did.' He held me for a long time before he brought me some cream to smear on to my grazes. After a cup of cocoa which I found hard to drink, we finally went to bed but did not sleep, hearing every sound in the night.

The following morning me and Billy were up earlier than usual and hurried to the canal. My body ached everywhere and my bruises were plain to see on my face. We found my clothes except for my coat and we hoped no one had seen us searching for them. They were dirty and some of them were ripped but my shoes were there.

'It must have been my coat that made the splash Billy. I heard it when I came round after the attack.'

Going to work later that morning was an ordeal. Seeing my friend from the mill with a couple of women I'd met the previous night, I joined them as we walked through the giggle gaggle and over the bridge on the canal.

'What happened to you last night?' one of them asked, 'you look as if you've had an argument with a fist or two.' My friend looked concerned. 'Has Billy beaten you Ruth?'

'No, of course not, I fell on the way home,' I answered but was reprieved from explaining as one of them pointed.

'What's that?' We all stopped and followed her finger. It was my coat half floating on the top of the water.

'Is it a body?' the other asked.

'I don't think so it's more than likely someone has thrown it away,' I commented as I couldn't think of any other excuse.

'I don't think so, not in these times dear,' replied the first. 'I think we'd better tell the police.'

'It looks a bit like the same colour as yours doesn't it Ruth? It could be a bit darker…but that could be because it's wet,' the second woman asked. I felt cold and sick. It was going to be very difficult keeping it secret.

'Yes,' the first one said, 'you were wearing yours last night…I saw you.'

'Well then, if you saw me wearing it last night then it's definitely not mine is it?' When did I learn to tell lies like that I reproached myself?

All through the day I thought about the night before and its consequences. Would I get pregnant? Who did it? Would he be watching me and maybe do it again if he had the chance? Most of all I wondered why me?

Going home from work we found the police at the side of the canal.

'Have any of you ladies seen anything unusual around here?'

The women stopped to talk to them but I made my excuses and walked on. When I arrived home I told Billy about the find in the canal and made him promise again he would not tell.

'It was a good coat, in fact your only coat. How can you manage without it?'

'I'll manage, if it means my secret is safe. I don't want people pointing at me and talking behind my back.'

Chapter 14

It took a while for the bruises and grazes to heal and each time I looked at them it brought it all back and made me feel sickly. I put cream on the grazes regularly, and Billy applied the cream to the places I couldn't reach with the hope I would heal soon. He was still angry and didn't try and hide it. It was a relief when the last one disappeared. Soon after, I began to suffer sickness in the mornings. Billy worried about this as my appetite declined and I looked pale and washed out.

'You know Ruth, you'll have to eat, you'll make yourself ill if you don't.'

'But I'm not well Billy. Food just makes me feel sick, even the sight of it. Don't worry about me, I'm sure it will sort itself out,' I pleaded.

'I think you'd better get to the doctor's and see what's wrong,' he begged.

'I'll be fine, stop fussing.'

I had a feeling that my worst nightmare was coming true. It worried me after that awful night but I couldn't even think about it. In my mind I hoped that if I denied it long enough it would go away, but pregnancy can't be ignored for long.

I went to see Dr. Harding and he examined me internally which hurt and frightened me.

'Are you and Billy happily married?' he asked.

'Very happy doctor.'

'You lead a normal happy married life,' he asked looking over his glasses.

'Yes,' I lied.

'All right then if you're sure.'

I thought about that, did he realise what he'd asked. 'Billy's my life,' I replied.

'Not for long my dear you're pregnant and I would say you've been in this condition for about four months. Now then sit down while we discuss this.'

The memory of that night returned again and again, plus all the horror it brought with it. Now, I would have the rest of my life to remember, my attacker made sure of that.

As I walked home my feelings were a mixture of dread and excitement. I didn't think Billy would be very pleased. At the same time I couldn't help but think…I'm going to be a mother. Who was the Father? Who could he be? If only I knew.

Billy went white with anger when I told him what the doctor said and he exploded with temper, threatening what he would do to the man if he ever found out who had done this to me.

'Please Billy, it's over and there's nothing we can do about it now. At least we'll be parents even though it's not ours. I'm sure we can learn to love it all the same.'

Billy didn't say a word but the anger in his face told me all I needed to know. It wasn't his and that hurt him deeply but there was nothing we could do about it.

'You don't want me to have an abortion do you Billy?'

'That's up to you.'

'Billy! I couldn't…and it's dangerous. Do you want to lose me?'

Billy replied by taking me in his arms and holding me tight. 'You know I couldn't lose you but I'm so angry Ruth.'

'Please try to accept it for my sake Billy. We'll put it behind us and try to be good parents. After all, the child is innocent.'

Billy kissed me gently. 'I know, and I'm sorry. Take no notice of me. Of course we'll make good parents.'

When I told Auntie Lizzie I was going to have a baby and it was due the following March, my Auntie was thrilled to bits and couldn't wait to write to Mary to tell her. As Billy had sworn Clem, his old friend, and me to secrecy regarding his war injuries, no one knew that he could not be the father. He did not wish to make it public because he said it would take his respect away. Auntie Lizzie told me that everyone did wonder about our lack of enthusiasm but it was dismissed with the thought that maybe we had been trying for a long time so couldn't believe it. Perhaps, she said, they thought, we were afraid of getting too excited. 'Is that right Ruth?' she asked and I reluctantly agreed.

I didn't carry the baby very well and I often had to go to bed when I finished work because I was exhausted. Mary wrote eagerly about what she was doing. She went into raptures of the experience she was getting but she was thrilled to bits with the coming birth and told us we must phone her straight away as Auntie Hilda had her own phone. So we took down the telephone number in preparation.

One of the neighbours gave me a pram with the promise that I would do some mending for her and Auntie Lizzie would make her a dress. 'I know it's supposed to be unlucky having the pram before the baby's born,' she sighed, 'but I have no room in the house to keep it. Have you got somewhere to put it love?'

'I'll keep it in the cellar until the baby's born, that should make it all right do you think?' I asked.

The woman nodded. 'I suppose so.'

Another of my neighbours read tea leaves, Maggie, and she would sometimes call on me and we'd shared a pot of tea. I had seen her stare at my cup after I'd finished drinking mine once or twice and felt uncomfortable at the thought of her seeing something I didn't want her to know but she never said anything. One day she sat and stared at it for a long time

'Can you see something,' I asked.

'Nothing I haven't seen before.' I felt on tenterhooks.

'What is it?'

'I'd rather not say.'

'You may as well. You're frightening me.'

'I'll say this Ruth…you have a dark secret, but that's all I'm saying.'

'What do you mean?' Maggie wouldn't say anymore and I was glad when she went home.

I thought about it for a long time. How could tea leaves tell that? Did it also tell her what my secret was? Impossible!

I knitted little cardigans with any bit of wool I could get my hands on, made do and mended wherever I could to save the pennies, holes in my shoes were covered with cardboard as the price of leather was too high to waste on shoes for me. I needed every penny for this coming little stranger. Auntie Lizzie confided in me that she hoped it was a little girl then I could dress her in little pretty dresses, but knew a boy would be just as welcome. I told her I didn't care as long as the baby was healthy. Auntie also made the baby nightdresses with any spare material she could find. I collected baby things from anyone willing to give me them in preparation and began to look forward, although with anxiety, to the birth. As I didn't know who the father was I also didn't know what to expect when it came to the colour of the hair, eyes and features and I often wondered how he or she would look when it grew. Would I guess then who the father was?

When I didn't feel well, those were the days that Billy became even shorter tempered. We knew we would find it hard when the baby came, as I was the main provider. I wouldn't be able to earn money to keep us as Billy still found it difficult to find work. His leg wasn't improving at all and his limp worsened. He didn't look well and he was obviously having a lot of pain. I worried about the future.

I did my best, or so I thought, to try and draw Billy into the excitement of the coming birth by showing him the layette my Auntie Lizzie was making. To say that she had used, what she called, bits of material left over from other things, they were beautifully done. Long nightdresses embroidered with feather stitch, little flannelette matinee coats and binders were all there ready for the day the baby was born.

When I was seven months pregnant I arrived home from work and found a note from Billy. Opening it I sat at the table and straightened it out.

Dear Ruth,

First of all, I love you so much but you know that. I just can't live with this any longer. I know you may think you will need me with you but what good am I? You'll have enough with the baby without looking after me. I'm sure you could find someone else to look after you and the baby much better than I ever could. I can tell that you're getting a little excited about the coming birth but my love; I don't feel anything at all except sadness that it isn't mine. How I wish that things could have been different but we can't plan these things. I found myself envying the man who attacked you because your baby should be mine. I hate it when you're ill and blame myself for not being there for you when you were attacked, as it was then when you needed me most.

Please find it in your heart to forgive me.

I shall always be yours.

'Together for ever'

Goodbye,

Love you

Billy

X X

After reading the note I hurriedly hid it away and ran out of the house arriving breathless and crying in my Auntie Lizzie's house. Auntie dropped her sewing and stood up.

'What on earth is the matter? You shouldn't be getting into this state in your condition,' she scolded.

After I told her about the note Lizzie asked to see it but I told her I'd thrown it in the fire. We went to search for Billy. It was raining heavily now and the cardboard covering the hole in the bottom of my shoes became soggy and uncomfortable. We called on friends and I even walked up to the top of the next street, as I could see the canal from there, but I couldn't see Billy. No one could find him anywhere. When I returned I found Auntie Lizzie waiting for me and she was crying.

'Have you found him,' I asked.

'Oh I, we've found him all right.'

I could feel my face drain of colour. 'He's not…de…' I began to sob.

'I'm afraid so.'

'Where is he?'

'Two of the neighbours have gone to collect him; they'll be here in a minute.'

'Where is he?' I shouted.

Auntie Lizzie sobbed 'He was in the canal.'

'Is he dead?'

'Afraid so love…why don't you sit down?' My Auntie put her arms around me and I sobbed into her shoulder. 'You have to be brave now for the baby's sake.'

'I curse, I curse…I curse…' I gasped for air.

'Nethen.' Auntie Lizzie comforted me as best she could.

They brought Billy home and I was devastated! We laid him out in the parlour until the funeral. Maggie came to see me and told me she had seen it in my tea leaves but she didn't feel as if I should know.

'Is there anything else I *should* know?'

'Not at this moment in time,' she grabbed my hand, 'but you'll get through it. Be brave.'

I collapsed that evening and the doctor was sent for. He ordered me to go to bed and have complete rest. Everyone who knew Billy was welcome to come and see him and we all agreed we would never have suspected he would do such a thing, especially with the baby on the way, but they didn't know the real reason. There were many tears shed. I thought of Maggie's words and tried to be brave.

When Mary heard the news she made arrangements immediately to come home. Auntie Lizzie stayed with me until Mary returned from London. We needed her now more than ever. Though I knew she had so much to tell us she was very good not to show it owing to the serious situation. Now she had to look after me and make sure the baby would be okay. Mary was determined to become an Auntie come what may she said.

On the day of the funeral, a quiet affair, only the immediate family and Peter, Jim's nephew, plus a few close friends came to the house for refreshments, although the church was full. Auntie Lizzie helped Mary make the sandwiches. I got up from my sick bed to go to the funeral and went back to bed as soon as we arrived home. I was broken-hearted. My first thought was to hold Billy's letters so I sought out the Angel Box and took them out. Lying in bed I read each one again then tucked them under my pillow. I didn't want to live anymore. I hated this baby, I hated my life and I wanted to be with Billy. My hand on my locket I eventually went into a fitful sleep. After a while, I awoke as everyone was leaving but I could still hear Auntie Lizzie and Peter's voice.

'You stay with our Ruth, I think she's going to need you Mary until after the baby's born at least. We'll have to keep our eye on her now.'

'Goodnight Aunt Lizzie,' both Mary and Peter called and I heard my Auntie shut the door as she left the house.

'Are you walking home tonight Peter?' Mary asked.

'You don't mind me staying with you for a while do you Mary?'

Everything went quiet after that and I drifted off to sleep again.

After a week of feeling ill and staying in bed, I went into labour. The midwife came and Mary made herself busy boiling water and being as useful as she could. I repeatedly shouted for Billy. Finally, after a long hard labour, the baby was born...a boy! At first, I wouldn't look at him, I felt as if he was to blame for everything. I wanted Billy...but I couldn't have him and it was all the baby's fault and I cried.

'Come on Ruth, you must hold him. He needs his Mam? begged Mary. It's not his fault that he's lost his Dad.

I thought about that for a while. It was true and goodness knows how it hurts when you find yourself unloved and unwanted. I knew what that felt like and it wasn't nice. It was the attacker that did this, no one else. I couldn't do that to the baby, the sweet unknowing baby who would never know who his father was. I sat up.

'Pass him to me,' I asked.

Pulling away the shawl that the midwife had wrapped him in after his bath I took a long hard look. He was very tiny with lots of dark hair and I looked into his deep blue eyes. No, it wasn't his fault. Not any part of it. But it wasn't fair. Life wasn't fair. The baby seemed to be capable of seeing right into my soul and I was sure he smiled up at me. I was hooked.

'Look at him Mary, he's beautiful. Aren't I clever?' and I knew I could never hold all the anger I felt and the tragedy we had suffered, against him. How sad his true father couldn't see him. Would he be proud? No, I didn't think so, not born under those circumstances.

'You're beautiful!' Holding his small and frail body against my breast I felt a sense of belonging all over again. He was mine, all mine alone.

I was told after the baby improved in health that the midwife took Mary on one side and told her the baby was far too small and it would take a miracle for him to live.

It seems that Mary gritted her teeth and vowed to herself that she would do her utmost to get the baby well. She thought I needed this child more than anyone in the world. It was my last bit of my husband and she would make sure she would do her best for her Sister and her baby. Bless her! She worked night and day taking naps whenever she could find the time, working on Auntie Lizzie's dressmaking business and looking after me and the baby and even through the night but she never complained. Soon I began to take over the duties of looking after my child and, although Mary didn't admit it at the time, she looked relieved. I could see my baby growing stronger.

'He wouldn't have made it without Mary's help,' I told Auntie Lizzie, 'I couldn't have managed on my own.'

'What are you going to name him Ruth? asked Auntie Lizzie, 'Are you going to name him after Billy?'

'I don't know. What do you think Auntie?'

'I just took it for granted that you would call him after Billy.'

'But then there's Uncle Jim too.' I thought aloud. 'He was always so kind to me.'

'I think you should call him whatever appears to be right for you. It's your choice Ruth, it's your baby.'

When I was left alone I thought about a name for my child. I didn't want to call him after Billy as he wasn't his father and I didn't think Billy would like it anyway. It would be nice to call him after Uncle Jim, especially now he was gone. I always liked Jonathon. Who would have thought that naming a baby could be so difficult?

Auntie Lizzie came round the following day. 'Did you decide on a name Ruth?' she asked.

'Yes, I have. I'm calling him Jonathon.'

'Where did that name come from?' asked Auntie Lizzie.

'I didn't want to name him after Billy. There would never be another Billy, so I couldn't name him after Uncle Jim either, it wouldn't seem right, so I decided on a name I always liked and that is Jonathon.'

'It's your choice like I said Ruth. If that's the name you've chosen then that's fine.'

One evening after going out with Peter, Mary came home alone.

'Where's Peter?' I asked.

'He's gone.'

'That's unusual.'

'He asked me to marry him tonight.'

'Mary, you have surprised me. You're a little young yet but…congratulations!'

'I told him no.'

'Why's that? I thought you would…one day.'

''That's it Ruth…one day but not yet.' I watched her for a while.

'You haven't refused him because of us by any chance, have you Mary?' Mary hesitated before answering.

'No, of course not.'

'You have, haven't you? Don't do this to me. I had a good marriage, there are no regrets.'

'I couldn't leave you now. How could I?'

'Oh yes, and then tell the world you couldn't marry because of me and Jonathon. Don't be silly.'

'Are you sure Ruth? Wouldn't you mind?'

'Not at all. You have to grab at happiness when you can. Now tell him you will marry him if that's what you want.'

'I will, next time I see him…as long as you're sure.'

'I'm sure.'

Mary went to bed looking much happier than when she came home that evening but Peter didn't call again and Mary never breathed his name.

'Why don't you go round to his house and tell him you've changed your mind?' I scolded two weeks later.

'Why should I?'

'Go to the shop then and tell him there.'

'I'm not asking him to marry me, it isn't my place. It just isn't done Ruth. He mustn't have been that keen or else he would have asked me more than once.'

'Maybe you hurt his feelings.'

'I think I've had a lucky escape, I can't see a future with someone who sulks every time he doesn't get his own way.' After that, I didn't say any more.

Mary didn't return to London to finish her college work. Auntie Hilda understood. We did hear not long after that Aunty Hilda had started seeing an old friend. I stopped writing to them and we eventually lost touch with her.

Things were really bad with lots of unemployment. Men and women stood at the factory gates waiting for bosses to come and choose them to work for the day. As soon as I was able I helped Mary with the simpler work and Auntie Lizzie tried to do her share too to help things along while Jonathon lay in his cot.

I talked to Peter sometimes when I went to Ashton for sewing aids and he told me he worked long hours as he loved the job and very much respected his employer. He visited our home when duty persisted to see his Auntie, but always kept well away from Mary. I often watched his face when she was around and his feelings were on show. How I wished that Mary wasn't quite so proud.

Jonathon was a sickly baby but after those first few months he improved and grew fast, becoming a sturdy young lad. I noticed, after bathing Jonathon and drying his hand that there was an unknown lump on his palm. I recalled the night on the canal when I was attacked and it worried me so I took him to see Dr. Harding. After he examined the baby he told me it was nothing to worry about. Dr. Harding gave it a name but I couldn't remember it.

'What does that mean exactly?' I asked.

'It's just a small deformity, that's all. Believe me Ruth it really is nothing to worry about. He's doing really well. Look at the little rascal.' He tickled Jonathon and the baby giggled. 'He's done so well.'

No wonder it didn't hurt my attacker when I pressed on it on the night of the attack, I thought. So it was a deformity after all.

Jonathon was full of mischief but he could get away with most things with just one smile. Everyone loved him and only I knew he had an unknown father.

People who knew Billy would say; 'He's a lot like his Dad, isn't he?' I would smile and nod my head. They would not, could not know any different.

As I pushed the pram around Ashton accompanied by Mary, I passed one of the beer houses and noticed they were advertising for a barmaid. It wasn't the best of jobs for a woman but things were hard and I knew if I didn't apply quickly the job would be gone. After asking Mary if she would take over putting Jonathon to bed in the evening I applied for the job then and there, explaining I knew nothing about pulling a pint but I got the job anyway and started the following evening.

A little dubious and wondering if I'd done the right thing I walked to work. The landlady, Clara, was very strict and gave me the rules. No drinking, no chatting to anyone in particular, always be courteous and when I was told by her to do something then I did it immediately. Her husband, Andrew, seemed very serious at first but after I worked with him a few evenings I realised he had a very dry sense of humour, if not a naughty one. The customers had a great respect for Andrew although some took offence until they got to know him better.

One of the regulars came in on this particular Saturday evening and Andrew spoke to him.

'I saw you out today with the wife and five children. Were they yours?' he asked.

'They were indeed,' was the answer.

'I never realised what bonny kids you had,' Andrew said.

The customer beamed all over his face. 'Aye, they take after their father,' he grinned.

'Oh, you know him then,' Andrew answered.

'Andrew…you'll get such a thump one of these days and there's nothing surer,' Clara shouted. 'Just behave.'

I looked at the man and noticed he wasn't smiling any more but the other men in the room were laughing and tittering amongst themselves.

It was hard work as most of the customers were men and they often made offensive remarks. On the whole, they were a jolly lot. Quite often I would find myself having to ward off their wandering hands too. They would tease each other and some of their remarks were extremely funny at times. Other times it would start a fight. After work I would walk home as I couldn't afford the bus fare. On occasion a man would try to walk me home or sometimes make a nuisance of himself. It was the last thing I wanted as it was late when I arrived home and I felt ready, so ready for bed. The job was okay as it did bring in extra money but I did miss putting Jonathon to bed in the evening.

Clara was kind in her own way and would pass on anything from the house she grew tired of. It could be a chair or even a cushion but everything was gratefully received. Also, when she heard that Auntie Lizzie and Mary made clothes she put in an order which boosted the kitty for us all.

Chapter 15

I tried so hard to make a home for Jonathon. Anything Clara gave me I would find a place for it and show it with pride knowing it was good quality as Clara didn't buy cheap things. As I wasn't good with a needle and could only do simple things like mending and darning, Aunty Lizzie would help me by doing the things I couldn't. I felt proud of my home and anything that could be polished, I polished. My step outside was donkey stoned on a regular basis and the windows cleaned. I hated doing the black leading of the fireplace as Billy always did that, but I did it. I also did home baking as it was cheaper and I had to make every penny count.

There were few men who entered my life and I didn't want any of them. There was no one to take Billy's place and I settled my mind to a life of living on my own with Jonathon. At least I had a job and my own home and as long as Jonathon was all right then I would be okay too. I would be in mourning for a long, long time.

I decided to go to Ashton market late on Saturdays and buy much needed groceries when they were at their cheapest. Putting Jonathon in the pram I pushed it to Ashton. When I could smell the acetylene lamps I knew I was close. The bright flames from the lamps were encouraging and gave me a warm feeling when we arrived at the stalls. I remembered coming for the first time with my Auntie and Uncle. It looked like a fairyland to me and Mary then. The man who boiled sugar and made sweets was still there but I didn't stop and watch him rolling it out now as I found the smell sickly. Jonathon was too young to realise what the man was doing so I walked by. The smell of Black puddings being cooked tickled my senses but I swiftly passed by that one too as I couldn't afford it. It was a shame as I could just picture one smothered with mustard and ready for eating. My imagination was too good as I felt hungry now, hungrier than before.

The man selling fruit was still there too. He was so funny and cracked jokes all the time making everyone laugh. I loved to stand and watch him and join in with the fun. He started with a number of oranges in a bag.

'Who'll give me a shilling for these?' he asked. No one put up their hands as they all knew too well that it didn't stop there. He then added apples and bananas and I found it all fascinating. 'Now then, who'll give me one shilling and three pence for the lot?' I smiled but passed on. I would have loved to buy his fruit but there was only so much I could afford and my money didn't extend to fruit.

I then moved on to the jewellery stall, where I looked but did not buy. Gold lockets were always my favourite and my hand automatically went to touch the one that still hung around my neck. Why did you do it Billy? I couldn't get my head around it. He should be here with me now. There was so much we had to share if only he realised. He couldn't have loved me like I loved him or he wouldn't have done what he did. Staring at the jewellery, the man must have thought he was going to make a sale as he came towards me.

'Can I help you?' he asked. I made my excuses and walked away. I must have been staring at the lockets while my mind was busy thinking of Billy. I must move on if only for Jonathon's sake.

I made my way to the inside market where the butchers auctioned the meat they hadn't sold. After buying enough to see me over the week-end, I pushed the pram back home.

My next door neighbour Mrs. Taylor, or Nellie as we became friendlier, was liked by everybody. Mr. Taylor, her husband was a different matter. He was flighty, and I, like many others, disliked him. He had a reputation for chasing women but the only one who wasn't aware of it was Nellie, or she shut her eyes where he was concerned.

I began to have problems with my back door. There had been a lot of rain in the past few days and it wouldn't shut very easily so I struggled to lock the door at night. 'It must be swollen,' I told Nellie.

'Jed'll fix it,' Nellie offered.

'Oh no! I'll sort it. Don't ask your husband. I don't want him to go out of his way for me.'

'No trouble,' said Nellie and Mr. Taylor came round the following day.

I liked Nellie and often felt like telling her just what her husband was like with women but I couldn't. I knew if Nellie found out then she would have a lot to say and I felt afraid she would maybe blame everyone else but her husband.

When Mr. Taylor came and knocked on the door I was reluctant to let him in. I did invite him in but felt uncomfortable and I was immediately on my guard. It didn't seem right he should be in my home when I was alone but he was obviously not aware of how I felt as he went into the kitchen and rolled up his sleeves. For a while I watched him without him knowing as I busied myself around the sink and cleaned the cupboard. He seemed to be intent on doing what Nellie promised he would, as he took a metal file from his pocket and began to fix the door.

'Would you like a cup of tea?' I asked. He nodded his head and I felt better having something to keep my hands busy. When he finished filing the wood he tried the door.

'Do you want to try it to see if you can use it okay?' He began to stuff the file back in his pocket.

I tried the door and it was fine.

'How much do I owe you Mr. Taylor?'

Mr. Taylor came towards me holding out his arms. 'Nothing…just you,' he answered. 'I know you're struggling so you can pay me in kind.'

I could feel myself blushing. 'I would rather pay you Mr. Taylor…in cash,' I answered as I went to find my purse.

He grabbed at me and we struggled. 'I know your sort,' he said, 'you give out the 'come on' then change your mind. You're just a little teaser.'

'Mr. Taylor I am not. I have given you no reason to think that.' He grabbed at my arm. 'Get off me. What would Nellie say?'

'You said you wanted your door sorting out just so that I'd come round and see to you. It wasn't that bad that you needed a man for that. You could have done it yourself but I can tell that you do need a man.'

'It's not like that. It was Nellie that offered your services.'

'It gets better. Good for Nellie. Why don't you call me Jed,' he replied, 'you know you want me.'

'*Mr. Taylor,*' I emphasized, 'leave me alone.' He was strong but I managed to push him away and stood gasping for breath. He came towards me again.

'If you don't leave me alone I shall tell Nellie,' I gasped.

Mr. Taylor grabbed me by the throat and pushed me until I could feel the sink pressing into my back. He brought his face close to mine. 'I know your sort. You're frustrated and needy and what's more…you're trouble. If you tell Nellie, I'll kill you.' His look was fierce and I felt terrified. Then his hands began to cover me everywhere. I was too afraid to stop him. Thankfully, someone knocked on the door but he ignored it. Then the knock was repeated and louder, so he quickly dropped his hands and turned to leave by the back door. 'Don't forget what I said,' he said threateningly. 'Don't you dare tell Nellie…or anyone else.'

I went to the front door and it was Nellie. 'Have you seen Jed?' she asked. I could feel myself getting hot. 'He left a few minutes ago.'

'Has he fixed your door?'

'Yes, its fine now, thank you Nellie.'

'You never know with Jed. He just disappears as soon as my back's turned. Doesn't tell me where he's going and how long he's going to be. I didn't know he'd come here, I just guessed.' Nellie went away shaking her head.

When I went back inside I could feel myself trembling from head to foot. I cautiously checked the house to make sure Mr. Taylor hadn't returned then breathed a sigh of relief. Going into the yard, I locked the back gate and to make doubly certain, I locked the back door and leaned against it. Now what? I thought. While Jonathon played on the floor with my pegs for the washing, I tried to collect my senses. How could I stop Mr. Taylor? Why does a man do things like that? Do I really look like a woman in need? I went to the mirror and took a good look at myself but I didn't look any different than before except maybe a little flushed.

I didn't need to worry as the gossip going around town was that Mr. Taylor had found a younger woman that took his fancy. He was seen out with her on the back row of the picture house. I felt sorry for Nellie. They had five children so it would be hard for her if they went their separate ways. Jed must care something for Nellie though or he wouldn't threaten to kill me if I told his wife the truth.

Mr. Taylor did try leaning over the gate one day to open it but I saw him through the window. Picking up the shovel, I quickly ran outside and gave his hand a quick tap with it and he didn't try it again.

After that I kept far away from Mr. Taylor and if anything needed doing by a man in the house I didn't tell Nellie.

In the afternoon I would sometimes go for a walk with Jonathon in his pram. Going to the park was one of the places I visited. There weren't many people about through the week so it was peaceful. If I took a book with me I could sit and read while Jonathon slept. The canal was close to the house so I would sometimes stroll along it to the swing bridge, which was the opposite direction from where I was attacked.

There were many happy memories here going back to when I was a little girl. The boat trips that were put on especially for the children stirred memories. They were unusual trips, where a coal barge was cleaned up and draped with white calico so that we children wouldn't get dirty. Memories of dark tunnels where boys would try and scare us girls and the drip drip of the water under the bridge. A man would walk up the tow path holding the reins of a cart horse that pulled the rope fastened to the boat while the children looked in awe at the water and some attempted to touch it, almost falling in. Then the trip home when one of the adults played a concertina and we all sang to the music. They were happy days, happy carefree days with no worries.

It wasn't a long walk along the canal to the bridge with not many people about, maybe an odd boat would pass by and the factory walls along part of it looked black with soot but it was peaceful. The canal was dirty and smelly but here I could think thinks out. There were many problems I had sorted while taking this walk and today was no exception. I would also come here when I felt low and think of Billy. It was good to get away for a little time, away from the problems of home and Mr. Taylor mainly. It still bothered me that he lived next door and I wished someone would put a stop to his shenanigans.

On occasion there would be men sat at the side of the canal with a fishing rod. I never saw any fish but I was told that once they were caught the fishermen returned them to the canal. It seemed a waste of time to me but as long as they enjoyed it, who was I to judge? Maybe they had problems to sort out too. I did notice many times when I walked over the swing bridge that the large fish in the canal seemed to congregate under it but I didn't like to mention it to the fishermen as I don't think they would have appreciated being told by a woman.

From the canal I pushed Jonathon up the hill. I sat on the grass at the top overlooking the canal for a rest. Jonathon was asleep. He looked so angelic and I hoped that he wouldn't turn out to be a monster like his father, whoever he was. What a pity Billy wasn't here. I felt sure he would have learned to love the child. This walk was calming me especially after my trauma with Mr. Taylor.

Another lady came and sat a little way away with a small girl who was about eighteen months old. I watched the child as she picked the wild flowers, then took them over to the lady, pushed them into her face for her to smell them, and then tottered off for more flowers. Eventually the lady got up and left the flowers behind. I looked around at the daisies and dandelions that were growing and looked forward to Jonathon picking me the wild flowers while I watched him as he chose each bloom. When and if Jonathon ever picks me flowers, I thought to myself, I'll put them in a jam jar on the window sill in the kitchen and feel proud that *my son* had chosen them just for me.

Chapter 16

Auntie Lizzie asked me to go to Ashton to get some buttons and beads from Kershaw's. They looked after Jonathon for me while I made a quick journey. When I arrived, Mr. Kershaw began to serve me. He owned his shop and worked in the business for many years. He bragged about Peter and how he'd taught him everything he knew. He said Peter was a willing young man and he was proud of his junior assistant as he helped the business to grow. He didn't mention that he was now desperate to find another assistant and he wanted to employ a girl.

Hannah Meredith applied for the job and she was a bright, cheerful young woman; also a kindly person and Mr. Kershaw told me when I called again how pleased he was with her enthusiasm for the work. He winked at me when he told me that both her and Peter were becoming very friendly and he encouraged their relationship. Before long, Peter and Hannah was an item and Mr. Kershaw congratulated himself with the fact that he was the one to introduce them.

'I'm so glad I had something to do with their meeting,' he told me one day when I called for some buttons. 'They were made for each other, don't you think?' Mr. Kershaw's face beamed.

I agreed with him as I felt I should but it hurt that Mary had missed the opportunity to work with Peter. If only I had realised there was a job for a girl at Kershaw's then I would have urged Mary to go for it. Hannah was a lovely girl but I wondered how Mary would take it when I told her that she was seeing Peter. After mulling it over in my mind for a while, I had second thoughts about telling Mary, deciding that things had a habit of sorting themselves out.

A new man began to collect my rent and he was really friendly. I looked forward to his visits every Saturday morning as he would sometimes stay for a cup of tea. If I had problems he was always ready to listen. The last man to collect my rent had been very business minded and surly. He would just walk in, take my money, sign the rent book and leave without speaking a word. Wilfred, the new man wasn't like that and it made a change after the other man left.

Dressmaking orders began to cool as Lizzie did less and less and Jonathon took more of their time. I asked Clara if she would give me an extra evening's work as it would put a bit more money in my purse and every penny helped the long hard struggle to survive.

Saturday evening was the worst night at the beer house as there were more customers to serve and sometimes they had too much to drink and could become aggressive. Uncle George came in one night with two women and they gave me a lot of grief. I found them loud and annoying.

'He says he's your uncle,' one of them said to me eventually.

'Did he?' I answered.

'Is he lying to me?'

George chimed in, 'I am her uncle.'

I turned round and said disgustedly, 'Only through marriage, that's all.'

One of them turned to Uncle George. 'I hope it isn't your marriage.' George laughed.

The women were demanding my time and being as awkward as possible. As I passed them by I could hear the insults directed at me, and Uncle George just sat and grinned at my discomfort. Towards the end of the evening, Andrew made a remark that Uncle George took offence to and he started a fight. Tables were knocked over as the fists flew then some of the regulars joined in to help Andrew. All in all it was pandemonium and I felt thankful when it was time to go home.

As I walked along the main street, my head felt as if a man with a hammer was beating it against my skull, then on top of all that I realised I was being followed. Painful memories of the canal filled my tired mind and I grew more and more anxious.

'Hello darling,' the man caught up with me and it was Uncle George.

'Leave me alone. I'm tired and feeling very short tempered tonight.' My footsteps quickened to try and make my point.

'I'm only talking to you, what's the harm in that?' he queried. 'I hardly ever see you now and you won't pass the time of day with me? Come on Ruth, be nice.'

'Where are the women you were with earlier? Go and find them I'm sure they'll be nice to you.'

'Wooo! Were you jealous?'

'No! Definitely not,' I answered.

Uncle George looked the worse for wear and kept leaning on me. I shrugged him off, attempted to ignore him and walked quickly still hoping he would get the message.

Nearing an entry to a back street, George came up behind me and placed his arm around my shoulders. I tried to manoeuvre myself away but as we reached the entry he attempted to drag me into it. I fought him and swore that my boyfriend arranged to meet me half way and he was big, very big and strong.

'There's no need to get nasty, I only want a kiss from my niece,' Uncle George pleaded.

'No you don't. Leave me alone. I've told you…my boyfriend will kill you if he sees you pestering me.'

Eventually, Uncle George believed me and as I walked away I could hear him shouting abuse after me.

'There are times when it's good to lie,' I muttered to myself.

Walking home seemed endless but I kept on the main streets and away from the canal. It was then I decided it was time I left Clara and her evening job. It was getting too late and too much for me to deal with and, if I was honest, meeting Uncle George that night had frightened me. The next day I called in to tell Clara.

'I had a man pestering me last night Clara on the way home, I didn't mention that I knew who it was, and it's frightened me a lot. I'm not coming back. I know you can find someone else to fill the vacancy so if you don't mind I won't do my notice.' I did feel guilty about it but I knew it was for the best.

'I'm sorry to hear that but I do understand. If you ever change your mind though then you can come back and work for me anytime.'

After that my rent began to get into arrears and Wilfred, the rent collector sympathised with me.

'I know life is getting difficult with losing your husband and then having the baby and everything but don't worry, things can always get sorted.'

I wondered how on earth things could get sorted when I had no job and there was hardly any work coming in for Lizzie and Mary. We pooled our food so if one had some then the others wouldn't go hungry but I desperately needed some work and money.

Every time I went out I looked to see if there were any shop assistants wanted. If I could only get a few hours a week it would help with the rent.

There were married men friends whom Billy and I knew that asked me to 'Just let me know,' if I needed anything and they'd give me a wink. I knew exactly what they meant and kept well away. If only Billy knew, but a good thing he doesn't, I thought.

I began to look for factory work but it was so difficult with having Jonathon, as I didn't like to keep asking Mary or Auntie Lizzie to look after him all the time. Not only that, there wasn't much going at all. The mending and darning I did didn't bring enough in. If I told Mary and Auntie Lizzie, I knew they would do their best to help me but times were bad for them too. Things got worse and when Wilfred appeared for the rent I apologised.

'I'm sorry Wilfred but I can only pay half the rent this week. I promise I'll pay it as soon as I can but things are getting a little difficult just now.'

'Don't worry Ruth. Do you remember me saying to you not very long ago that things can get sorted?'

'Yes, I do. Although I couldn't for the life of me see what you meant with that.'

'Couldn't you?'

'No, what did you mean?'

'I can pay it for you,' he offered. I was horrified.

'I can't let you do that, why should you?'

'Well...I was thinking of payment for a favour.'

I thought for a minute, this could be my lifeline. A bit of washing and ironing for him, I could do that and I wouldn't mind at all.

'What's that Wilfred?'

He stood up and came over to me then bent down to kiss me as his hands began to explore my chest. I pushed him away.

'Get out.' I jumped up and pointed to the door. 'I'm not that hard up that I need to sell my body.'

'Oh c'mon Ruth, will it be such a hardship?'

'I thought you were my friend...I never learn.' I felt hurt.

'Oh c'mon. Jed next door said you were up for it. I thought there was a chance for us to get on better but you've blown it. I shall need to put pressure on you from now on I'm afraid...unless you change your mind,' he threatened.

'You can do your worst but I'll have none of that so get out.'

He left the house and I broke down and sobbed. What a fool I'd been. I never realised he was getting the wrong idea from my hospitality. Oh God, what an absolute idiot I am. I would be sure to never to do that again and never trust another man for a long time. What was the matter with men? Were they all the same? They see a woman on her own and think she's fair game. How dare they? Well, this girl isn't for playing so they'd better get that into their thick skull.

After that I made an appointment to see Ernie Walker, the owner of the property.

Calling round to my landlord's house I walked up the path between lawns and flower beds to his front door and knocked. Ernie opened it and invited me in. His house was a great improvement on mine as it was in a much nicer district for a start, and his house overlooked the park. No orange boxes here but solid well polished furniture. He invited me to sit on one of his well upholstered chairs and I sank into the leather cushions that were stuffed with feathers.

'Now then Ruth, what can I do for you?' he asked.

'I'm sorry to bother you but I wondered if I could come and pay you directly here at your house? Would you mind?'

'Well, it's unusual but if you prefer it, I don't mind. Is there something bothering you that makes you want to pay me direct?'

'I'm glad you asked me that. You see, I'm having problems with the rent just now. I'm struggling but I promise as soon as things improve I will pay all my arrears to date, I really will.'

'Is that right?'

'I promise I will.'

'I thought at first that you'd come to tell me that Wilfred weren't behaving himself.' My face must have shown my true feelings. 'Am I right Ruth?'

'What makes you think that?' I asked.

'I can tell I'm not wrong. Are you going to tell me that I am wrong?'

'I don't want to tell you anything other than what I've already said,' I answered in embarrassment.

'Okay, if that's what you want. I know you've always paid on time and I've never had much trouble in the past of receiving your rent. I can understand what you're going through so I'm willing to let things go…for a while.' I was aware that he wouldn't allow me to leave my rent for too long.

'Thank you so much. I don't make empty promises Mr. Walker, and I do promise to give you everything I owe you eventually.'

'Okay, Mrs. Masters. I'll bear that in mind.'

'Thank you Mr. Walker.' I left.

Making my way back through the park I sat on a bench. It had been a relief to talk to Ernie and I felt glad I decided to take that route instead of having Wilfred calling on me. I never wanted to see that man again.

Two weeks later, I noticed there was another rent collector making the rounds so Ernie Walker must have known all about what Wilfred was up to. Maybe he'd already had complaints.

Not long after that, while visiting Ashton, I saw a notice in Kershaw's drapers shop, 'Wanted, part time shop assistant.' Knowing Mr. Kershaw, I entered and asked about it. Peter was there and showed his enthusiasm with me to his boss so after asking me a few questions Mr. Kershaw offered me the job.

'Well young lady, its three mornings a week and more if we get busy. I have a lot of respect for Peter and if he says you'll be okay for this vacancy then its okay with me.'

'I'll need to check with my family but I can't see there being a problem.' I thought about how Mary would take it.

Feeling a little apprehensive, I made my way home and dreaded having to tell Mary as I knew that one thing would lead to another and she would find out about Hannah. How I wished Mary had told Peter how she felt. It was hurtful to me that the love Mary felt for Peter and given up for me and Jonathon hadn't been necessary. Now it was too late.

Mary took it well, especially as she knew I was feeling the pinch with not having much money coming in. She agreed to keep her eye on Jonathon while I worked the three mornings. I called in to see Mr. Kershaw again and told him.

'That's fine. If they say it's okay then just come in and start right away in the morning.' Now I had a day job so that would help and I could pay a little more on my rent.

One day me and Mary were walking in the park and saw Hannah out with Peter but Mary hurried away before they looked in her direction. I watched her figure disappear with the pram while I stopped to pass a few words with the loving couple.

Before long, the shop became empty next door to Kershaw's and Mr. Kershaw bought it. Hannah having shown an interest in hats gave him the idea to extend their wares to millinery. Hannah proved herself and the business thrived. Kershaw's business grew.

Both Peter and Hannah ran the millinery side of the business. Peter thought they should not only sell ladies hats but men's too. Mr. Kershaw looked proudly on them both and allowed them to do their own thing and the couple became very close. Then Mr. Kershaw's health began to deteriorate. Peter began to manage the shop for him and his boss was rarely seen again behind the counter until finally he died. I didn't go to work again for a while as Peter told me they were closing until further notice.

After the funeral, the will was read and as Mr. Kershaw had no family, he left everything to Peter. I walked past one morning and saw Peter through the glass door of the shop and knocked. He opened the door for me.

'Hello Ruth, it's nice to see you. How's the family?'

'Fine thanks. Sorry to hear about Mr. Kershaw.'

'Yes, he was a good man.'

'He was; he left you everything didn't he?'

'He did but I shall miss him dreadfully. There's so much to do I don't know where to start.'

'Can I help?' I asked and Peter breathed a sigh of relief.

'Would you?' and I nodded.

'He's not only left me the shop but his house too. Do you know where he lived?' I shook my head. 'He lives in a big old terraced house where he was brought up, and he was the only child. When his family died he carried on living there alone.'

'He left you that too!'

Peter nodded. 'It has a lifetime of souvenirs to go through and that's going to take ages. There'll be boxes and boxes…I don't know what to do.' I touched his arm.

'You know I'll help you all I can Peter.'

We walked through the shop, looking and poking into boxes and I could see that Peter had to stop himself from getting too emotional whenever he found something personal of Mr. Kershaw's. There was a knock on the back door and Peter opened it. It was Hannah. He invited her in and she gave him a hug.

'I know you haven't asked me to come in this morning but I felt I should. You sit down and I'll make you a cup of tea.' Hannah went for the kettle but I got there first.

I smiled. 'Would you like a cup of tea Hannah?' I asked. I thought it was time I left them alone and grabbed hold of the kettle. 'I'll make the tea while you keep Peter company.' Hannah smiled at me and nodded. She understood.

Wiping his eyes on the back of his hand, Peter allowed Hannah to lead him to a chair. Bringing in the tea a little later, I found the girl knelt on the floor at his feet and looking up at him.

'We will miss him Peter but we'll get through this.' As an afterthought, she added, 'together.' He kissed Hannah gently on the cheek.

I left and drank my tea in the kitchenette to give them a little privacy but I could still see and hear them.

'Hannah, I've been doing a lot of thinking since he left me the business.'

Hannah looked up at him and whispered, 'Yes Peter.'.

'I know it's not the right time really but…will you marry me? I have plans for this place and I need you by my side.'

'Oh Peter, of course I will.' Hannah stood up and threw her arms around his neck.

'Ruth,' Hannah called, 'we're engaged.'

I came in and congratulated them both but they didn't realise the tears I shed were for Mary and what could have been.

'But now my future wife,' I think we'd better open the shop, we have a business to run.'

'Tomorrow.' Hannah skipped to the front door of the shop and turned the card to read, 'Open' then scrawled onto a card to stick underneath, 'Tomorrow.' I didn't have the heart to tell her that she should have put the day as it could be misunderstood.

Throwing open the door wide Peter called 'Come on you two, let's have a look at the window and see if we can make changes for the better.'

Peter stood outside as we walked out to join him, his eyes met mine and for me it brought memories of when he proposed to Mary and the sadness that came after. Deep in my heart I hoped that they would both be happy and Mary would find someone else that she could love as much as she loved Peter. Although I felt sad that he hadn't proposed again to Mary, at least he had chosen well, after all, they did share their work and I did like Hannah.

Me and Hannah helped Peter to sort everything in the shop and then began to help with the house when we could. It was a rambling six bedroom terrace with a large back garden which had become overgrown. In the garden were bushes that needed to be pruned back but would bloom again soon and would transform the garden. There was also an apple tree that stood tall.

'That would give you shade when it's warm,' I said. When we came to cut back the overgrowth we found an unusual bench. It must have been very old but it was still very useable, handy too when we became weary and this we put under the apple tree. The house was packed crammed with memorabilia from way back. If Mr. Kershaw hadn't been such a nice man it would have been very interesting but there was so much sadness felt with everything we handled, it was nothing else but a chore.

His furniture looked solid and capable for anything. It needed polish but would look as different again with a little care. There were carved chests, grandfather clocks, grandmother clocks in mahogany and oak. There were so much it took us a while to get things ship shape. Then there were the chandeliers and brasses to clean.

Peter asked me to start work on a regular part-time basis again. He needed help with what to throw away and what to keep and after he married, we discussed what changes we would make and finally decided a dressmaking service would do well.

'We need someone to take over this side of the business, don't we Hannah? Do you know anyone Ruth?' asked Peter.

I thought about it for a while. He knew Mary's work. Was he hinting that Mary could be interested? I knew things were a little tight at home as people were a little more careful at spending their money so there were fewer orders for Auntie Lizzie and Mary to do.

'I know a good dressmaker Peter.'

'Well then, who is it?' Hannah asked.

'Mary!'

Hannah's smile froze on her face. Her mood was light hearted until she heard the name.

'Is she free?' Peter asked. I nodded. 'That's wonderful Ruth. Do you think she would come and work for us, only I know she has her own business to consider?' Peter sounded eager.

Hannah had met Mary a number of times in the shop and I guessed she had become a little jealous of her. Peter often spoke of her in glowing terms and maybe she felt threatened.

'It's up to you of course Peter if that's what you wish,' Hannah's voice then fell quiet but Peter didn't notice. I realised the thought of seeing Mary on a regular basis pleased him but obviously not Hannah.

'I know she works well, it may be a good outlet for her to sell even more of her work. Plus…' Peter looked eagerly at Hannah; 'it would bring more business our way.'

He visited Mary that evening and laid out his plans. Mary mentioned she knew a girl who would maybe help her if necessary. Mary and Peter discussed the business and after Peter went home, Mary and I decided it was best to take a good look at what Peter had to offer. So the following morning, leaving Jonathon with Auntie Lizzie, we visited the shop.

Although Mary had visited the shop before, her dealings with Hannah had been brief as Peter always insisted on serving her himself. Today, she was in her company for a while and later told me that she found herself liking the woman. They had a lot in common and they both liked a challenge. Mary agreed to their business deal and hoped she had made the right decision. After, Mary and I walked home.

'How did it feel seeing Peter again?'

'I have seen him a few times before.'

'Yes, but not on your own like today when he showed you the room upstairs. Do you think you'll like the job?'

'Why not? It has possibilities.'

Mary started to organise her room upstairs at the shop. Peter bought two sewing machines for a start. All the material, buttons, cotton and anything else came from the shop below. Hat shapers, feathers and all sorts of adornment for hats needed to be ordered as we were offering this special service. Jonathon started school and if at any time when he wasn't at school and Lizzie couldn't look after him then Peter allowed him to come to the shop. It worked very well.

Orders began to come in and sometimes Mary made a hat to match the outfit or I would take one from the shop and she would alter it to match, if that is what the customer required. Hannah did her part by taking orders and her enthusiasm with the customers was second to none.

Peter looked after the shop and I took over the orders and bills and helped to serve the customers whenever needed. It was one of these days when Alfred walked in.

Chapter 17

I gave Alfred a big welcome smile as it was lovely to see him again. 'How are you Alfred? I haven't seen you for ages. How's life treating you?'

'Okay thanks, and how's married life?' he replied.

'I'm a widow Alfred, but I do have a son. His name is Jonathon and he's gorgeous and I love him very much.'

Alfred looked shocked. 'I'm sorry, I didn't know Billy died. How did that happen?'

'He drowned.' I didn't give him any details and decided to change the subject quickly. 'I have Jonathon, so I can't grumble too much. Anyway, what about you? Did you marry?'

'No, I never did.'

'I'm sorry to hear that.' At the same time my heart missed a beat and I wondered why.

'Father died, but Mam's okay.'

'I'm sorry! Your Dad seemed really nice.'

'He was. He left me the business.'

'Oh, so you're a business man now?'

'I suppose so, in a small way. The only thing he stipulated was that I must always give my younger brother a job, and make sure he was okay, but that goes without saying anyway.'

'Of course. Are you still living in the same house adjoining the business?'

'Yes, we still live with my Mother.'

'It's lovely to see you again but,' I looked at the clock on the wall, 'I must get on with my work or I'll never get home tonight.'

'I'm sorry, I didn't realise.' He took a button out of his pocket. 'Have you six buttons to match this one please I? I'm always losing my shirt buttons.'

When I left the shop later it came as no surprise to find Alfred waiting for me and looking his best. He fell into step at my side and walked me home. By the time he left me at my door it was as if we had never parted, and I still liked him.

We arranged to meet again in two days time.

When I went to bed that night I realised how lonely life had become without Billy. I could never love anyone again like I loved him. Would Alfred understand this? Only thing to do was to see how things developed.

We were doing really well in the shop and employed two more women to work upstairs. There were ladies with money to spend, or maybe their husband's money. Hannah began to feel unwell and developed a bad cough. We blamed it on the hard work. It went worse and it took a lot out of her. Mary would find herself taking over while Hannah went to rest quite often. Hannah's enthusiasm declined as did her energy. Picking at her food she began to lose weight. This went on for a while and then she began to stay home and leave the shop to Mary.

'Hannah has lost interest in the shop, she's lost interest in everything, and I don't know what to do.' Peter seemed helpless and Mary tried to console him.

'She's not well Peter. I've watched her over the past few weeks, and she's been in work when she should have been in bed. You know as well as I that she should see a doctor.'

'But she won't. I've insisted at times but she's absolutely refused and made such a fuss that I had to give up for fear of making her worse.'

I saw much more of Alfred and I eventually introduced him to Jonathon. Week-ends would be spent with my son as I didn't want to confuse the child and I had to be sure of Alfred before things went that far.

Mary helped Peter more than before as she took on Hannah's business and Peter employed another girl to do the work upstairs that Mary supervised. After leaving work Mary often went home with Peter and made a meal for both him and Hannah before she left to come home. Hannah's temperature seemed high one evening and Mary wanted to call out the doctor but Hannah wouldn't hear of it.

'I'll be all right, please don't make a fuss,' was all she would say.

Mary would call on me on her way home and tell me about Hannah.

'I feel so helpless Ruth. What can I do? I hate to see her like this and its killing Peter.'

They would ask Mary to stay and have a meal with them but she always refused. Hannah began to cough blood but asked Mary not to tell Peter as she didn't want him to worry. Mary asked Hannah again if she would allow her to call Dr. Harding. After feeling really bad and not eating all day Hannah finally relented. It was bad news…she had Consumption but insisted on staying at home and begged Mary to look after her with Peter. Her weight went down until she became so thin Mary said you could see her bones and with no appetite they knew there wasn't much chance for her to live much longer. Mary worried about Peter catching the disease.

I called to see Hannah and she did look ill. Mary and Peter sat with me at the side of Hannah's bed. Hannah was asleep and her face unrecognisable from the happy carefree girl she once was.

'How long is she going to suffer, Mary?'

'I don't know but I hope for her sake it's not much longer. I worry about you.'

'Why?'

'Because you could catch it.'

'I don't have that much close contact with her,' he whispered.

'You don't?' Mary looked up at him.

'No, I stopped that after...' He stopped in mid sentence and we could see he was deep in thought. 'It must have been when I first suspected the disease.'

'Poor Hannah and poor Peter.' Mary covered his hand with hers and gave it a gentle squeeze.

By now Alfred became a regular at my home and took Jonathon to his heart. I began to enjoy Alfred's company even more. Soon he took Jonathon fishing, and then he would help to put my son to bed at night. If a room needed decorating, which they all did on occasion because of the damp, he would do it and always made a show of going home reluctantly.

We went on holiday together and stayed in a boarding house, separate bedrooms of course, to Blackpool and sat on the sand in chairs while Jonathon played with his bucket and spade. I loved Blackpool with the fresh air and promenade and it took my mind back to when I first caught sight of the sea. I made a pretence of falling asleep but my mind was busy. What were my feelings towards Alfred? Jonathon seemed to love him and that was a good sign. He is caring and I could do worse, I knew that. Opening my eyes very slightly I watched him as he played with Jonathon.

He took Jonathon paddling and I sat up to watch them jumping over the waves and laughing. When they returned, Alfred made sand castles and other things with the boy and in the evening, in my bedroom at the guest house, he dropped to his knee and proposed marriage for the first time but I felt reluctant and declined.

'Jonathon is too young yet Alfred, I would rather wait until he's a little older.' It was an excuse as my only experience of relations with a man were with my attacker and my blood still ran cold at the thought. Sometimes I even wondered if I would ever get over it.

'I'm a patient man Ruth and I know what I want. What's more, I know you're worth waiting for so I'll keep asking and you can't blame me.'

'Thank you Alfred, I appreciate that.'

'But you know Ruth from what you've told me, Billy ended his life for you, so he wouldn't be a burden and stop you from enjoying what you had. He must have loved you a lot but then so do I. Think seriously about this and realise why he did what he did. It was for you to live…to live Ruth and not in mourning.'

When we returned home, Mary was excited and couldn't wait to tell me that she heard the news the council were building houses on Clarendon fields which were closer to the park and a nice quiet area.

'I'm told they will have electric installed and hot and cold water…and a bathroom. Oh Ruth they sound ideal.'

Both Mary and I went to the council offices and put our names down hoping for the best. Rents were to be higher than what we already paid but it would be worth it as the houses we had were both damp and bad for our health. Council houses were more modern so we wouldn't need a tin bath hanging up outside that would need to be brought in and filled with water that we had to prepare first. No going out in the cold to use the lavatory too and there would be light at the flick of a switch. Also, there would be gardens so we could grow our own vegetables and maybe a few flowers. We couldn't wait to hear if we were successful and made plans for if and when we were. It was a while before we learned I was successful and I looked forward to moving into the two bedroom terraced house with Jonathon. At least I wouldn't need to keep on my toes regarding Mr. Taylor.

Alfred proposed again and I refused yet again. 'Why won't you marry me Ruth? You could move in with the family or we could live in the council house with you, when you think about it that would be a great beginning to our marriage.'

'No Alfred, I'm not ready yet.'

'I gather you didn't give it much thought after I proposed last time.'

'I did Alfred, I really did. It's just that I would rather wait until Jonathon's a little older like I said. Let's wait until he's ready to accept you as his dad.'

'You're using your son as an excuse aren't you?'

'Please Alfred, let's change the subject.'

He helped me to move into the new house and Jonathon did his best by carrying the small things. It was an exciting move, after the gas mantles we'd been using; it appeared very bright with the new house having electric. We wouldn't need as many matches because electric lights didn't need them; it was just a flick of a switch. I went through the house turning the lights on and off. It was so easy. The fireplace was large with a back boiler to heat the water too and an oven which was a little more modern that our old one. No more boiling the water to have a wash and we had two taps, one for hot and one for cold water on both sinks and the bath. It was fantastic! No more having to empty the bath by hand as we had a plug in the bottom we just pulled out and let it do it itself. Great! It was all there. Everything we needed. The stands for me to place the pans over the fire and the oven to cook my pies, I couldn't wait to get cracking. The coalman came and delivered three bags then Alfred lit the fire with some wood he had brought with him.

There were two bedrooms. The front one I claimed and I set up the back bedroom for Jonathon. When I took Jonathon to bed that night, he was exhausted. I thought I would have trouble settling him in but I didn't as he fell fast asleep straight away. When I went back downstairs, Alfred gave me a small parcel.

'What's this,' I asked.

'Open it and see for yourself,' he replied.

I ripped off the paper and revealed a box, a long box.

'It isn't...?'

'Open it and see,' Alfred urged.

I opened the box and found a beautiful ladies' watch with a silver strap.

'Is this for me?'

'Well, it isn't something I'd wear myself.'

'Why, it isn't my birthday?'

'Almost every time I've seen you, you've been wondering about the time so now you'll know exactly what time it is.'

'Alfred, that's lovely and thoughtful of you.'

He took it out of the box and put it on my wrist. I looked at it and stretched up to kiss him.

'Thank you,' I whispered.'

'It was worth it.'

I found the kettle and Alfred filled it and then made a drink while I unwrapped a few things. After he'd emptied his cup, he pulled on his jacket.

'I'll be off now Ruth. Will you be okay?'

'Yes Alfred and thank you.' I kissed him goodnight and he left.

I couldn't wait to try my new bath so I went into the bathroom and filled the bath then after stripping off my grubby clothes I sank into the water. It was delightful. Jonathon was asleep in bed and I was alone. Oh Billy, you don't know what you've missed, I thought.

Jonathon loved the garden even though it was a mess. At least he had somewhere he could play without danger and it belonged to him alone. Alfred came over when he could to work on it until there was a little order with paths and separate beds for vegetables and flowers. I relied on Alfred so much. He put up pictures, chopped wood for the fire plus many other little jobs that I found difficult.

Mary heard soon after that she was successful too, also with a two bedroom terrace house. Mary moved hers and Auntie Lizzie's things in when she could with help from Peter. Alfred helped too and did his best to get her settled in. Auntie Lizzie did what she could and we soon had it looking spic and span. We didn't live in the same street but round the corner from each other, even within waving distance from our back gardens.

Alfred bought a new car so took me and Jonathon for a drive into the country. It was a lovely day and reminded me of the day my Auntie and Uncle took us for a walk to a farm. Knowing how much I enjoyed the fresh milk that day, we sought out a farm and called for a glass of milk each. It was as I remembered, absolutely delicious and still warm. After a while we rested while Jonathon played. It was good to see my son enjoying the fresh air with plenty of room to run around without getting under everyone's feet. Alfred spoke about when we married and if and when we had children. It made me feel guilty but I was still afraid of what marriage would bring. Could I cope with it and more children? After a while we made our way home.

As we walked on stepping stones over a stream, Jonathon fell in and was soaked through. Alfred went in and picked him up, carrying him to the side and laying him on the grass while he took off the child's shoes and stockings. He stood him up and took off his shirt and shorts and everything else, and then taking his clean white handkerchief out of his pocket he began to dry the boy as much as he could. I took off my petticoat and wrapped it around Jonathon, and then Alfred picked him up and carried him back to the car.

As Alfred drove us home I watched him from the corner of my eye. He was a good man, a thoughtful man and I was very lucky. He always had time to spend with Jonathon and showed him patience. When I needed anything he would go out of his way to help. What was it with me? Why couldn't I return his care?

There were many men looking for work and leaving their families at home to find it. Cotton mills and the pits were always taking on new blood. Some of the pits didn't have a good record as there were explosions with lives lost so the men had to be replaced.

Auntie Lizzie moved into Mary's bedroom so they could take in a man as a lodger, Jed Harrop, who was looking for work in one such pit. His wife and two children followed and all their family shared the same bedroom so they were soon overcrowded but it helped with the rent. At least they had their own bathroom so they could all bathe once a week. Jed kept the fire stoked up for the hot water to make sure. No having to fill the bath up with buckets. Now they had taps that did all the work for them and they didn't even need to empty it with buckets as they only had to pull out the plug. There were still many going to the town hall for a bath and to do their weekly washing so there were no grumbles from anyone at home when they had to wait their turn for a bath. Jonathon also had playmates too whenever we called.

It took a while before I took on a lodger and it was a young newly married couple. Arnold worked in the mill and Jane was a clerk in the same mill. They were easy to get on with and they took over their share of the chores.

Jonathon was a little shy at first with them but over the next few months he grew to love them and they loved Jonathon and would look after him if I needed to go out some evening. It worked very well for us all.

Arnold was interested in gardening and with my permission began to grow vegetables. He would spend many hours turning the soil and weeding where necessary. It was good for me as I was given fresh vegetables straight from the garden and they tasted especially good. His cauliflowers were the biggest I had ever seen and I counted my blessings. Later, Arnold asked if he could have a few hens at the back of the garden. The eggs would be welcome and so I agreed. Soon there was a roll of chicken wire to put up for the pen and Arnold brought home some wood from goodness knows where and began to make a little hut with nest boxes, helped by Jonathon. A dozen chickens were bought and placed in the pen. As the chickens grew, I had second thoughts as each morning at the crack of dawn there was a cock-a-doodle do. Arnold admitted that he, as far as he knew, had bought only female chickens but the cockerel had sneaked in somehow. Still, Jonathon loved the chickens that were produced through the mistake and any male chickens were killed for the table as soon as they were big enough. Arnold would allow the child to play with one on the odd occasion but he taught him to be gentle so that he wouldn't hurt the baby hen. Every day, the boy would help Arnold collect the eggs with growing excitement at each one found. Only thing was that when Jane cooked the mash for the hens, the smell of the potato peelings cooking on the gas ring was enough to put you off your meals but it was worth it all really if it was only just for Jonathon's sake. The boy would play for hours in the garden talking to the hens and chickens and digging for worms.

Flowers were the next thing that Arnold decided to grow, so a plot was made close to the chicken run. He put in Michaelmas Daises, Golden Rod and a few roses plus other roots that had all been generously given by neighbours. One rose was especially beautiful, pink and perfumed and I admired it.

'I've called that Ruth,' Arnold said, 'for some reason it reminds me of you.'

Close by was a red rose. I looked at it and thought of the day when I came home and found the roses on my dining table. I stood looking at it for a while remembering it all over again. They looked the same as the rose that was now growing in my garden.

'Do you mind if I name this rose Arnold?'

'Feel free,' he smiled. 'What are you going to call it…Jonathon?'

'No,' I answered, 'not this one. This one is a special one to remind me of my late husband. I'm calling it Billy.' I thought of the poem Billy had written and recited it in my head. 'And if we part, an invisible cord no one could sever, will keep us both 'Together forever,' so even in the garden we'd kind of be together.

Arnold didn't mind me helping myself to the flowers and sometimes brought a few in for me. Billy's red rose I picked, but only one, and placed it in a pickle jar alone. I set it on the window ledge in the kitchen. Sometimes I added the pink one too. Now I had occasional fresh flowers in the house and it didn't cost a penny. Life was beginning to look good.

On a bright sunny day I would sit outside the back door with Jane and watch Jonathon play and help Arnold. Sounds of the chickens gave me the feel of the countryside and I loved it.

Jonathon loved the caterpillars he found on the cabbages and would ask me for a jam jar to put them in. I didn't mind until one day he brought them into the house without me knowing and left them at the back of the table with no top covering them. No one noticed until we found caterpillars crawling all over the kitchen.

Alfred called on one of these days and helped us to find all the little creepy crawlies. 'Do you think Jonathon would like to go to the zoo tomorrow? I thought it would make a change for you both. At least he would be unable to put them in jam jars.'

'What about the business Alfred?'

'Don't worry about that, it's about time I gave Alex something to do, and he is quite capable of handling things while I'm away.'

The crow of the cock awoke me the following morning and I climbed out of bed and drew the curtains. Looking out of the window I could see a grey sky and hoped that the rain wouldn't spoil the day.

'We won't let the weather ruin our visit to the zoo, will we Jonathon?' and the boy squealed with excitement. 'It's going to be a perfect day for the zoo; we'll make it so won't we? And Jonathon nodded his head in agreement. 'Alfred will be here soon in the car so I want you to be a good boy and eat your breakfast then we can get ready. Will you do that for your mam?' Jonathon nodded his head again.

I was ready early and repeatedly checked the time with the town hall clock which I could see from the back bedroom window. Even though I wore the watch that Alfred gave me, I was always unsure whether or not I had wound it, and didn't like to risk breaking it by over winding it. I felt as excited as Jonathon when Alfred rolled up in the car. There was a picnic I had already made and I looked forward to seeing the boy's face when he saw the animals, especially the elephants.

Jonathon didn't let us down and viewed them all with great excitement. At first he was a little taken aback at the elephant, it was so big he was mesmerised.

The birds didn't seem to thrill him quite as much but we took him round to see them anyway.

We all enjoyed the picnic in the gardens and ate everything I had prepared. Later, we went into the café as we were both ready for a fresh cup of tea and Jonathon was given a drink of milk.

We visited the fun fair and put Jonathon on a little merry-go-round, standing and waving at him each time he passed. Later, when I went to bed, I took out the angel box I kept in a drawer in the bedroom and opened it. Reading my letters I came to the last one I received and sat with tears running down my cheeks at his last words. Tucking them under my pillow I lay with my eyes shut thinking of how much Billy had missed and still couldn't understand why he left us. Hopefully I would dream of him telling me what to do regarding Alfred, but I didn't dream at all.

Alfred took us to Blackpool two days later for a three day holiday. There was something about Blackpool that always gave me a special feeling. Maybe it was because it had been the first time I saw the sea; I don't know, but it definitely had something.

We stayed in the usual boarding house, Alfred in a single room and me and Jonathon in another. We spent time on the beach making sand castles and paddling. Jonathon squealed with delight each time a wave went over his feet. Then we walked the full length of the prom. After that bracing air we went back and almost fell into bed.

I felt sad to go back home as I really enjoyed being with Alfred. It was nice having someone who cared for me again plus he was so good with my son. Jonathon thought that Alfred would be staying with us when we got home so it was beginning to get difficult.

'Mam, why do my friends have dads and I don't?' he asked the following morning at breakfast.

'You had a dad love but he went to heaven to be with Jesus,' I answered.

'Why mam, didn't he like us?'

'You weren't even born then. If he'd have seen you I'm sure he would have stayed.' I could see Jonathon frown as if he was thinking about that for a while.

'He didn't like you then mam?' he asked.

'Yes, of course he did but it was his time to go.'

Changing the subject quickly I asked 'Would you like to go out to play? The sun's shining and you can play in the garden and find some worms for the chickens.'

Jonathon ran outside and I, after making myself a cup of tea, sat at the table and began to think of what Jonathon had said. Did Billy really fall out of love with me? Maybe that was his trouble really and not the fact I was pregnant with another man's baby.

A few days later we heard the sirens coming from the pit not far away. As Jed was working at that time, I hurried to the pit head along with, what it seemed the entire town. Everyone seemed to be going in the same direction. We found when we arrived there had been an explosion and ten men were trapped. No one was sure whether or not they were alive so there were men already down there trying to get to them and bring them up to the top. Jed was one of those men and I breathed a sigh of relief. I felt awful. I knew there were men still trapped but I couldn't help but be grateful that Jed wasn't one of them

We all stood about and waited for news. Finally, they all came up alive. Two men were badly injured and taken off to hospital but the other eight weren't too bad and just had cuts and bruises. Everyone praised Jed and how hard he had worked to release the trapped men, but he wouldn't hear of it.

'We all played our part, no one more than anyone else,' he claimed.

Mary worked hard at the shop especially now that Hannah couldn't and I looked after Hannah with a little help from a part time nurse who Peter employed through the day. The Harrop's took over the upkeep of her house with Auntie Lizzie's help but as my Auntie was weak, they did most of everything. Sometimes Mary would stay up all night with Hannah then snatch about three hours sleep before going to work at the shop. At least Aunt Lizzie had a meal ready for her when she did arrive home which was always late. It began to take its toll as Mary began to look ill with the lack of sleep and the hard work. One night after I took over from Peter at Hannah's bedside, Hannah passed away.

We closed the shop until after the funeral. Peter couldn't cope with the shop and Mary couldn't do it without him. It was heart-breaking.

The morning of the funeral, it rained heavily which made it even more sombre. Peter was very distressed and held on to Mary's arm as if he'd never let go. The church filled with mourners at her funeral as she was well loved. There were many came back to the house for the sandwiches and tea and all spoke in whispers. When they left, Mary and I with a little bit of help from Auntie Lizzie cleaned up then prepared to leave.

'We're going now Peter,' Mary said. 'Lock the door after us and go to bed. You've had a hard day so get as much sleep as you can.'

'I wish you would stay tonight Mary.' His eyes were pleading.

'You know I can't. Goodnight dear.' We heard him close the door behind us. I breathed a sigh of relief that it was all over. It had been a hard, long day and we all felt drained. Now Mary's biggest worry was getting Peter through it all. He would find life very hard and she couldn't help too much or tongues would wag. I truly hoped he would be strong enough to get through it.

As we walked home Mary worried about leaving Peter on his own and the following morning admitted she hardly slept that night.

When Peter and Mary finally opened the shop again we didn't realise how much there was of Hannah around. It took them all their time not to break down but we finally got through the first day.

'Are you still coming home with me for tea?' Peter asked Mary.

'No Peter. It's something you must do for yourself now.'

His eyes filled with tears and she touched his arm. 'People would frown on us spending time alone together so soon after the funeral. You know what they're like; I bet they were suspicious before so we don't want to stoke the tittle tattle.'

'You're right. It's just that the house will seem so empty now.'

'I know, I know.' My heart went out to them both but Mary knew she couldn't do it if they didn't want to feed any rumours. Unknown to him she watched him walk away from the shop.

'Look Ruth. He's not the man he was. He looks like an old man the way he's bent over and he's so troubled. I feel I should run after him but I know I can't.' It was sad but too soon. She didn't want the reputation she knew people would give her if they were seen going to his home together.

Chapter 18

Business as usual but it was difficult. Peter found trouble concentrating and his personality became so different. Gone was his sense of humour and the customers commented on his serious disposition. It was all understandable, of course, but it wasn't good for business. Mary and I attempted to keep the shop up to standard but it was difficult for her too. I worried about Peter and so did Mary, enough to ask me to accompany them to his home so that we could make sure he received a good meal. It was difficult for me but I agreed, so for at least twice a week we made him a meal together and wouldn't leave until we had seen him eat it. He complained but he knew we were doing our best so he did what he was told and ate it.

Peter began to change again and his sense of humour returned. Both Mary and Peter knew they held feelings for each other but didn't speak of them. It was taboo until at least a year after the funeral of Hannah.

Mary went out with friends and Peter took up bowls and tennis. Mary would go to watch him alone when she could and sometimes helped with refreshments after. Sometimes Peter would have a female partner. Mary admitted to me that she would watch the woman throw her arms around Peter if they won and try not to feel jealous, but admitted there were a few pangs of jealousy, even though she knew there was nothing in it. It was hard for both of them to keep their feelings hidden but it just had to be.

I would often invite Peter for Sunday lunch where he would join Jonathon, Alfred, Mary, Jane and Arnold for the mid-day meal. We women would all go in the kitchen and prepare the food while the men stood outside discussing the country's problems while looking after Jonathon if it wasn't raining. Then after the meal and the dishes were all clean and put away we played card games stopped only by making and eating sandwiches and drinking tea.

Sometimes Jonathon played with his toys and sometimes he joined us. When Peter and Alfred came to leave they would kiss us and Mary looked forward to Peter going home but for that reason only. I could see the soul searching in their eyes and thought again how cruel fate can be.

Peter hired a daily to keep things clean and tidy. Slowly the business returned to normal. Ladies fashions were changing. Big puffed sleeves were out. Hairstyles were changing too and a bob was becoming fashionable. We kept busy but we still talked of Hannah although it was becoming less painful.

The Charleston hit the dance halls and the young ladies were throwing their legs about like they'd never done before. Skirts were becoming shorter. Everything was changing. Jonathon often asked me if Alfred was going to be his dad but I always avoided the question. Knowing he would make a good dad, my past still made me hold back. I would sometimes look hard at Jonathon, trying to find a resemblance to someone I knew or even a stranger that I knew by sight but I couldn't. It was difficult to try and place someone with the same characteristics. Who had such dark curly hair? I could only think of Seth and that was impossible, but I didn't know of anyone else.

Jonathon became ill. He had a temperature and lay down most of the day. I went to the chemist to see if I could get a bottle of something. Walking into the shop I rang the brass bell on the large wooden counter and waited for old Mr. Harris to come from the back room. I liked to come here as it always had a special kind of smell. Perhaps it was a mixture of all the medicines and potions. Even the wooden drawers full of dried leaves and whatever a chemist has in them could add to the smell. I looked around at the large glass bottles, some of them were full of coloured liquid and I didn't know what that was but it looked impressive. All the wooden drawers lining the wall at the back had brass knobs and I wondered if someone polished them and how often! Old man Harris appeared and the questions in my mind were forgotten.

'Yes, and what can I do for you young lady?' He had a funny squeaky voice and he always made me smile when he spoke but I managed to keep a serious face.

White hair stuck out on each side of Mr. Harris's head like you would expect from a mad professor as he looked at me over his spectacles that were perched on the end of his rather large nose. His moustache was long and unkempt, while his white overalls always looked starched and spotlessly clean, even though his pockets always bulged with something or other.

I explained Jonathon's symptoms and Mr. Harris disappeared into the back behind a curtain and returned clutching a bottle of black medicine.

Pushing it across the sturdy wooden counter he whispered, 'That's three pence. Now if he gets worse then call for the doctor.'

'Why's that? Won't it cure him?'

The white moustache twitched as he spoke, 'There's a child with pneumonia down the road and...well, you never know.' He squinted at me with his grey eyes. I paid him and left, clutching the bottle and hoping this would make Jonathon better.

Soon Jonathon came out in a rash and he didn't get any better but worsened then he started to complain about his sore eyes so I had to call out the doctor. He quickly diagnosed measles so at least it wasn't pneumonia. I had Alfred bringing the boy's bed downstairs where it was warm and we drew the curtains to protect Jonathon's eyes. Alfred was the one who stayed up all night to watch over Jonathon when he became really poorly.

'You'll need your strength through the day to look after Jonathon,' he insisted and talked me into going to bed.

'But what about your work?' I asked.

'Our kid can do what's necessary for now.'

Auntie Lizzie always said that you should keep covered up well and kept warm even though you have a temperature but I didn't agree. I told Alfred to try and keep the child cool by wiping him down with the flannel after wetting it with cold water when he was burning up. He tried to keep Jonathon's face cool like I asked even though I could tell he didn't agree with me. He also gave him drinks when he was thirsty through the night, plus kept the fire going too. I felt very grateful. Sometimes I would awaken to the sound of Alfred chopping wood for the fire and it gave me a warm feeling inside. He would also make me a drink of tea when I came downstairs for my breakfast.

Arnold and Jane were good with me and Jane kept the house clean. Whenever I had to go out then Jane, Arnold or both would watch over Jonathon. Finally, Jonathon's temperature began to drop and he began to improve.

Alfred took us out in the car to the countryside where Jonathon was free to play. He loved taking off his shoes and running in the grass but I worried about him getting cold.

'Put your shoes and stockings on Jonathon, that's a good boy,' I shouted, but Jonathon turned a deaf ear.

Alfred chased him and Jonathon ran off giggling until Alfred caught him and twirled him round.

'Don't Alfred, he'll be sick,' I called then realised my worrying stopped the boy from being a free spirit and enjoying himself.

'Am I being silly, worrying about Jonathon like I am?' I asked Alfred and he nodded his head.

'I can understand you but he loves this. Look at him. He has roses in his cheeks and he's laughing. I haven't heard him laugh like that for a while.' I had to agree with Alfred, he was right. When we came home Jonathon began to play with his toys and only then did Alfred suggest taking us for a holiday.

'I'll take you and Jonathon anywhere you'd like to go now he's improving. The lad needs some fresh air in his lungs and you both need to do a bit of convalescing Ruth,'

'I don't know whether I can. I'll need to ask Peter if it's okay with him.'

Peter didn't object. 'I think it's a good idea. It will do the lad good...and you.'

The next time I saw Alfred, I gave him the good news. 'Where shall we go,' he asked. 'Where is your heart's desire?'

'I think Jonathon should have a say in that, don't you?' Alfred agreed.

'Let's go to Blackpool? Please, please.' Jonathon pleaded. 'I love Blackpool.'

On the first day we battled the wind when we walked along the promenade and Alfred took off his jacket and put it around Jonathon's shoulders to make sure he wouldn't catch cold. The boy looked ever so proud wearing a man's jacket. It was too cold to sit on the sand so we took Jonathon into the tower. We danced together in the ballroom holding Jonathon's hands and he loved it. Later, we went to the pleasure beach where we allowed him to go on a ride, waving to him every time he passed us. When we arrived back at the guest house we were all ready for our meal. Later that evening we took Jonathon to the pictures, then went back to go to bed. Jonathon looked so much better and the colour returned to his cheeks as I kissed him goodnight.

This time the stay in the guest house made me feel uncomfortable. I felt that Alfred must be wondering why I was so aloof and refusing to marry him. He was so considerate with both Jonathon and me that I could feel my defences slipping. There were so many men that wouldn't have waited for me like Alfred had. It was time I answered yes to his next proposal as I didn't want to lose him.

I lay in bed for a while thinking over the past. Billy was the love of my life even though we never fully shared a bed. It was very sad that he couldn't have been Jonathon's father. Life is cruel the way it twists and turns. How I wished I had been a little more giving when I went with Billy. Maybe he'd wished that too. There were times when we both came close but stopped before it went too far. Then the war and our time were over with no more opportunities to seal our love. Who had taken my virginity away? Which faceless man had dared to take Billy's place?

Alfred was right in what he said. Billy, bless him, did end his life to make mine better. He didn't know the effect it would have on me, he couldn't see that clearly. All the same he did it for me and I have lived in mourning ever since and that wasn't Billy's plan. I felt sure in my mind that the next time Alfred asked me to marry him my answer would be yes.

The next day the sun shone, so it was down to the beach. Alfred bought Jonathon a bucket and spade and helped him to make a sand castle with a moat. The tide wasn't too far away so Jonathon filled his bucket with water and brought it back repeatedly to fill the moat. He couldn't understand why it kept disappearing.

I watched Jonathon and wondered what kind of father Billy would have made. I was sure he would have been a good one but then again, if he couldn't get over the fact that Jonathon was the child of another man, then maybe not. It was something I would never know. After all, he did take the coward's way out. Gosh! How could I think that of Billy?

After a while Jonathon began to play with another boy who was with a family who sat close to them. When the family began to make their way to leave, I overheard the lady say, 'Now go back to your mummy and daddy and perhaps we'll see you again.' I thought, so that's how we look to others…like a real family.

A short time after we all decided to go for a paddle. We left our shoes and stockings with Jonathon's bucket and spade and walked along the beach allowing the water to cover our ankles. It was cold but soothing. Jonathon would stop at times to pick up a pebble and throw it further into the sea. Alfred and I held hands and for the first time in my life I felt part of a family. As we had no towel with us, Alfred came to the rescue again and used his handkerchief to wipe all the sand off Jonathon's feet before putting his shoes and stockings back on. We left our shoes off until we went back on the promenade then used our stockings to wipe our feet before putting on our shoes. It was uncomfortable having sand still stuck on our feet as we couldn't get rid of it all. My feelings for Billy, I had often thought, would never happen again but my feelings for Alfred were turning to real love and Jonathon loved him too. I would always love Billy and never forget him but I was beginning to move on. I began to realise that I couldn't live in the past as I still had a future and I must live it, if only for my son. Jonathon looked so pale while he was ill and so listless, now it felt good to see the change in him. It was a much healthier child that returned from Blackpool from the one who went on holiday.

Alfred and I became closer after the holiday. I was seeing him in a different light. Maybe I was getting over the man who had ravished me at last. It was still vivid and sometimes gave me nightmares but I knew there were many men who didn't treat women like that. Alfred was kind. He even stopped the car on the way home when we passed some swings because Jonathon asked him to. My problem was that I couldn't remember much of my own Father but remembered too much of my Step-father before the fire. His memory scarred me for life and I never wanted to marry a drunk or abusive man. Alfred wasn't like that and I didn't believe he would ever change. Now I must look forward to the future and I knew now I had found the right man to share it with.

Returning home I felt a little disappointed at things returning to normal. I missed being with Alfred and wondered why I had kept on refusing to marry him. Thinking about it, I realised I had loved him for a long time but wouldn't accept it. With my mind littered with bad memories and still thinking of Billy too, I had been too wrapped up with my grief. Now I must push it all behind me and look forward.

Walking down the street with Alfred, I began to link his arm, much to his delight. Whenever there was an excuse to put his arm around me, he did, and I didn't object. He stayed later in the evenings and spent more time at weekends with us. He seemed to belong as a family and I waited for him to propose again but he didn't.

Chapter 19

Mary and I were walking home together from the shop deep in conversation when we heard a rumpus and noticed two men fighting in front of a public house. There was a crowd around urging them on.

'Ruth, it's Uncle George,' Mary said as we drew close.

I could see who it was but preferred to ignore it. The men were fist fighting and rolling over and over on the grass watched by the crowd both from the pub and passers by. Mary stopped to watch so I was forced to do the same.

I overheard one man say, 'He did pinch his beer, I saw him.'

The man he was speaking to answered, 'George is always doing that. He's pinched mine before today but you think twice before accusing him.'

'I know what you mean,' said the first man, 'he has quite a reputation.'

'I only hope this fight will cure him but I bet it doesn't.'

'No, he always comes out on top does George.'

The fists flew and we could hear the sound of them hitting bare flesh and bone. The fight ended when Uncle George finally knocked the other man out. The man was sprawled on the floor with blood over his face and Uncle George began to kick him as he spat out filthy names. Some of the other men that stood around grabbed hold of Uncle George and threw him against a wall, holding him there and whispering threats until his temper subdued.

I heard the second man utter, 'It's a pity it isn't George on the floor, he might stop pinching our beer if someone gave him what for.'

Mary and I walked away and as we did, Uncle George wiped the blood away that trickled down from his nose with the back of his hand. I stood frozen to the spot and my eyes opened wide. There was a lump, a large lump, in the palm of his hand. A lump I never noticed before but was now very prominent. Jonathon's lump was on his other hand but it was too much of a coincidence. My mind returned to the canal and what happened when I became pregnant with Jonathon. So this was Jonathon's father? His hair was the same colour and naturally wavy too. Why hadn't I realised before? This was my husband's murderer. How could it be? Not Uncle George! He hardly noticed me and Mary standing there and I preferred not to speak to him at this moment.

'C'mon Ruth, stop staring and let's go home,' Mary urged. 'Don't forget, Auntie Lizzie is looking after Jonathon.'

I couldn't remember getting to Mary's house where Auntie Lizzie had a meal prepared for us all; I couldn't remember eating her meal. Even when Jonathon sat on my knee I just reacted automatically but my thoughts were elsewhere. I stayed for a short time after the meal and helped Auntie Lizzie and Mary with the mending.

'Mary, has Uncle George ever made a pass at you?' I asked.

Mary put down her work and looked at me quizzically. 'What on earth made you ask that?'

'Has he?' Looking at Mary's face I added 'I'm only curious, that's all.'

'No! Why, has he made a pass at you?'

'No, of course not.' I answered as if it was an absurd question.

'He'd better not have. He's a bad one that one,' Auntie Lizzie remarked.

'I'll tell you something though Auntie Lizzie,' Mary said, 'our Uncle George can fight. What a dirty fighter he is too. I wouldn't like to cross him.'

'When did you see him fight?' Auntie Lizzie asked.

'On the way home, you should have seen him. After he knocked this man out he was kicking him while he was on the floor.'

'And you, poor soul, are related to that?'

My blood ran cold. No wonder I was battered and bruised that night. I felt as if I'd been kicked a few times. After watching him fight today it was quite possible. Thank goodness he didn't kill me I thought to myself.

After Jonathon and I reached home and he was put to bed, Arnold and Jane showed me a letter they received from the council. They were very excited because they had been allocated a council house not far from me so they would know a few of their neighbours already. I attempted to show them my enthusiasm but I felt nothing as my mind was still on Uncle George and the night on the canal. Arnold and Jane decided to play a board game and asked me if I would like to join them but I said I wanted to read a book that someone had given me and wanted returned shortly. It wasn't like me to lie but I couldn't concentrate on anything tonight and I didn't feel like talking to anyone either.

I pretended to read the book while the couple played their board game but my mind was full of other things as I went over and over the night at the side of the canal. Did Uncle George know it was his niece he was attacking? Maybe not, it was dark, and if he had been lying in wait for someone, he may not have recognised me. Then again…he always wanted me…but then again he seemed to want every girl…

That night was a long, long night for me. My mind was on the canal side and what happened, most of the night. Had he seen Jonathon and realised it was his son? Did he care! I didn't think so. Could I remember anything more to be sure Uncle George was my son's father? Why had he thrown my coat in the canal? Come to think about it, he must have scattered my clothes too as I found it difficult to find them. Was he watching me and laughing at my embarrassment? He must have known I was a virgin. Had he told anyone? Had anyone made fun of Billy? Did Billy know that someone knew and is that why he ended it all? My mind went over and over this all night. Eventually, morning broke and I felt happy to leave my bed. However, I knew there was only one thing to do, I would go and see Uncle George and ask him outright.

All the following day I could think of nothing else. Working was all done automatically and I was glad of any lull in the shop as I wasn't my usual self with the customers. Even the figures weren't adding up and I had to repeat my additions all the time. As soon I was alone with my thoughts again then Uncle George would come to mind. Would he admit it? Would he attack me again? Was I doing the right thing going to see him? That evening, not telling Mary and Auntie Lizzie where I was going, I asked if they would look after Jonathon for a few minutes as I had some business to attend to. Without looking up from their work they agreed. I pulled on my jacket and made my way to Uncle George's house. It wasn't far but already I felt as if I shouldn't go any further as there were warnings flashing through my head.

As I walked closer to his house my heart began to thump hard in my chest. My belly felt as if lightening was cutting through and I was going hot and cold at the thought but I carried on, I had to know. It was time I knew.

It was dark when I arrived at the house. I noticed his curtains looked as if he'd tried to draw them but they weren't wide enough. There was a rather large gap between them. Perhaps he wasn't in. Should I give up and go? No, I would see it through now. Looking through the gap in the curtains, I thought I could see him sat in a chair with its back to the window. I gripped hold of the metal knocker on the door. BANG, BANG, BANG. I made a positive noise. No turning back now I had to know the truth. I waited and nothing happened so I gripped the door knocker again. BANG, BANG, BANG. I made sure that if he was in he couldn't ignore me. Eventually, he opened the door slowly and stood there, his hair tousled, chin unshaven and stripped to the waist. His pants looked as if he had been locked up in them for weeks.

'What do *you* want?' There he was again, leering at me. I hadn't imagined it after all.

'I think we need to talk.' I stood as tall as my small frame allowed.

'Then you'd better come in.' He opened the door just enough for me to get through. He gave a mock bow and then straightened, sweeping his arm to the side to allow me to pass then he slammed the door behind me. 'Now young lady what can I do for you?' He looked down at me and I felt vulnerable and very uneasy. I looked around the room which was dark and unkempt. The table in the middle of the room looked as if he hadn't moved the leftovers from a few meals and they were now going mouldy and smelling.

'Sit down…if you want to.' He added as a challenge. I pushed some of his stuff to one side and sat on an old chair. His home smelled dirty and it was, and the stench of stale tobacco and beer was unmistakeable. An ashtray on the table was overflowing with spent cigarette ends and ash.

'I am honoured today.' Uncle George said with sarcasm as he sat on the chair he'd been sat on before.

'Look, I've got to know. Did you ever ravish a woman on the canal side four years ago?' He sat looking at me for a while and a sneer started at one side of his mouth then gradually took over the rest. He jumped to his feet.

'Me? I don't have to ravish anyone. I can find plenty of *willing* women.' He looked me up and down as he walked round me. 'Mind you, I wouldn't mind having you; you have a lovely body…nice tits too. I've always fancied you.'

'Oh shut up! You're my uncle for God's sake.'

'Only through marriage, you've told me often enough. Oh come on Ruth, just a quickie,' he laughed and I felt disgusted.

'Don't you ever think of anything else?' I felt angry, so angry my body burned with it.

'You brought it up.' He gave a sickly laugh, 'Now it's my turn.' He looked down.

'For God's sake, think Uncle George; it's really important to me. It was you weren't it? You beat me that night and took advantage of me.' Uncle George was still standing, grinning at me with that evil look in his eyes. 'That woman you ravished that night was me. It was me you bloody fool and I have a child from that night. Did you ravish me? Were you the one?'

'You mean…I have a little bastard? Well that's a turn up for the books, isn't it, eh! Me and you are the parents of that kid I've seen you with?' He stood and laughed at me. 'Fancy that eh? Me a daddy to your little brat,' and he laughed again. Grabbing my arm he began to push me towards the stairs. 'C'mon, I've got a few minutes, perhaps we can make another.' His hand began to grope me over my blouse and I pulled my arm away from him.

'Get off me and leave me alone.'

He made a grab for me again and I began to fight him off and wished I had never bothered finding out about Jonathon's birthright; after all it wasn't good news. Uncle George grabbed hold of my chin and forced a kiss on my lips. I felt sick and pushed him away. He slapped me in the face.

'C'mon, what are you fighting for; I've had your body before.' He tore at my clothes.

'No!' I didn't want this to happen again. What had I done? He was pushing me to the stairs then had a change of heart and attempted to force me to lie down where I was but I was struggling and fighting back. No, I wouldn't lie down and make it easy for him but he was too strong. It was happening all over again. He held my hands behind me as he pushed me against the table. My fingers felt something; I wriggled them and felt a blade from a knife. My hand closed on the handle. By this time he had ripped my skirt and was pulling it up. I struggled to free my arm and I lifted and plunged the knife into his chest with all my might as I was weakening. He took Billy's life as sure as there was a moon at night with his actions and I hated him for it. Uncle George let go of me and dropped his hands. He looked at me with shock passing over his face.

'You little bastard you've bloody stabbed me.' I looked up at him, watching, wondering what he was going to do next as I realised the knife hadn't done much damage as I could still see most of the blade. I hadn't been strong enough and the blade wasn't sharp enough. His arm came up to his chest and he pulled out the knife then threw it to one side as the blood began to trickle down. The knife was familiar; where had I seen it before? I remembered now, it was at the side of the river when Mary almost drowned.

'That knife, it was you weren't it that killed that man? The man in the big house. You, you…murderer. It was you, wasn't it? I recognise the knife. Was it you?'

'Shurrup you bitch! You don't know what you're talking about.' He stood up to his full height and lunged forward. I made for the front door. As I reached it I felt his hand grab my hair and he pulled me back. 'Now then bitch. How do you like this then?' He pulled me towards him and then threw me across the room and I landed heavily on the floor. He came over to me and pulled me to my feet. I fought him and he punched me a few times until almost unconscious I slipped to the floor where he straddled me and began to rip the top of my dress. Still fighting him with the strength I had left, I could feel the wet sticky blood on his chest as he came close. I was scratching his face, and he laughed as he began to tear at my clothes again.

'You're wild…and I like it.' He rubbed his face over my neck and chest and I could feel the stubble scratch and hurt. I noticed the knife close by and made an attempt to grab it but Uncle George got there first, lifted his arm and plunged the knife into my left breast. 'How do you like it...whore?' he sneered. I began to drift into blackness and couldn't feel my body anymore but I was aware of his hands around my neck...he was squeezing, squeezing; I could feel myself slipping away. As I drifted in and out of consciousness I thought I heard voices from far away. .

'You bastard! I wondered where you were. I should have known when you didn't turn up you were with another woman. You swine! Open this door. I'll kill you, you...you...you bastard!'

Uncle George released his grip on my neck. 'Bugger off,' I heard him call.

'Open this door...now,' the voice demanded. 'Or else I'll break your bloody window. I'll get in somehow and I'll kill you...and her.'

I felt as if I was floating above as Uncle George stood up and I drifted off for a few minutes again, then I heard the same voice.

'Let me in you pig.'

'Go away. It's off between us. I don't want you.'

'I can see that. Sod you. I have my pr...' I drifted off again and then I heard a door slam.

I felt my skirt being lifted as I drifted in and out of consciousness. There was a loud knocking on the door that disturbed me.

'I've told you to go away,' Uncle George shouted.

There was a lot more banging and voices. 'Open this door...now,' someone called.

Uncle George left me. More banging then a loud noise and I opened my eyes to see Uncle George run past me. I closed my eyes again. My head was throbbing and I couldn't see clearly. I thought I'd imagined it.

'Oh my god!' A voice disturbed me and I opened my eyes again. A policeman was bending over me and he had something in his hand, it was a handkerchief. He was placing it on my chest and whispering to me.

'You'll be all right love. Don't move. I'll get an ambulance.'

There was someone else in the room. They were both talking. I saw Uncle George and it looked as if he was handcuffed. I came round again and attempted to speak.

'Don't try and talk,' the policeman said. 'There's an ambulance on its way.'

'No, he...he...he tried...to strangle...murder me.' My voice was a painful whisper. 'The knife.'

'I should have finished her off; she's already told you hasn't she?' I could hear Uncle George mutter.

'Shut your mouth,' the policeman tugged at George's handcuffs and George shook his head.

'That knife. I'm a bloody fool. I kept it because I liked it…stupid!'

The ambulance came and took me away to hospital. They told me later that Uncle George was taken to the police station watched by the neighbours but no one called round to tell Auntie Lizzie and Mary.

Chapter 20

Jonathon cried for me it seems but then he would, after all I was always there for him. Mary worried herself sick she said as she walked up and down searching high and low for me. I should have told them where I was going but you don't realise until it's too late.

Mary told me later that after calling at my house she asked Arnold and Jane if they had seen me but, of course, they hadn't. They dropped everything though to help to find me. Like they all agreed, it wasn't like me to not tell anyone where I was going. Mary walked along the canal a way before she went back yet again to check whether or not I had returned. When the lamplighter came down the street she finally took Jonathon to a neighbour's house as Auntie Lizzie still wasn't back and neither were Arnold and Jane. Mary asked the neighbour if she would keep her eye on Jonathon while she went to the police station.

Later, as Mary left the house to catch a bus, she saw Alfred drive past on his way to see me. Running back to my house she called him.

'You're just in time Alfred. If you want to see our Ruth then you'd better come with me to the hospital.'

'Why, what's happened?' Mary said that Alfred was concerned.

'Ruth's been taken to the Ashton Infirmary. There's been some kind of accident, although the policeman did mention assault. I just don't know until we get there,' Mary said she explained as best she could.

'I…I don't understand,' Alfred stuttered.

'I don't know either, an accident or assault but Ruth mustn't be very well if they've taken her to hospital. We'd better get a move on.' Mary urged him to hurry.

Alfred said, 'Jump in the car, I'll drive there.'

Mary said it was eleven-o-clock that night by the time they saw me at the hospital. They could see my face was very bruised and swollen and the bruises from Uncle George's fingers on my neck were plain to see.

I remembered that I found talking very difficult and the constable kept asking me what happened. After he asked me a few questions the nurse intervened.

'I'm sorry constable but she can't answer any more questions. The poor woman has had enough. Come back tomorrow after she's had a good rest.'

'You poor, poor girl.' Alfred looked upset and Mary said she followed the constable out of the ward and asked him what happened and how did I get into that state?'

Alfred hardly ever left my bedside except for when the matron told him he had to do but he returned as soon as he was allowed. Mary kept Auntie Lizzie informed.

After a few days Mary told me what had happened. 'Going into the police station made me feel as if I was expecting the worst,' she said. After I gave the duty sergeant the details, the policeman looked very serious. He said do you know anyone by the name of George Lewis? And I said he's my Uncle. He said, is it possible that your sister could have visited him today? And I said it's possible but highly improbable as neither of us like him very much. He said I think it's highly probable that your sister could have gone to see him. Then he asked me to hang on and told me to sit on the bench that was against the wall.'

'I'm sorry Mary to have given you all so much worry.'

'It's not your fault. It's that damned Uncle of mine. Anyway where was I? Oh yes, the policeman picked up the telephone and dialled a number. He asked for the sister and my heart sank. Honestly Ruth, my mind was in turmoil.'

I shivered at the thought. 'Oh Mary, I'm so sorry.'

'Don't be silly Ruth.' Mary carried on talking. 'I thought, has our Ruth had an accident? Surely I would have heard before now if she had. Then he started talking to the sister and he asked her if you were awake after the assault. I was horror struck and I thought assault? who could have assaulted you? Everybody loves you. Then I remembered they mentioned Uncle George. I thought surely it couldn't be Uncle George. I bet that woman in hospital isn't my sister.'

'I know what you mean, it is unbelievable.'

'I know. I heard him ask if you could have visitors and then he told me you were here and on Ward two and we weren't allowed anymore than two visitors at a time. He also told me you'd had an accident. After that he spoke to the constable so I left. Then I went and picked up Jonathon and went home. I informed Arnold and Jane that you had been found but wouldn't be home. They were all concerned and asked where you'd been. They said they'd searched everywhere but no one had seen you. I told them that everything would be explained as soon as we knew what had gone on. By this time Auntie Lizzie was home and she told me to go to the hospital and see you and she'd look after our Jonathon as she couldn't handle it, it would upset her too much.

'Tell Auntie Lizzie not to worry. I'll be fine.' Poor Auntie, it must have been a shock for her. 'Last night when you came, my eyes were closed but I could hear you talking. I was drifting between sleep and awake and I heard you Mary say, they've obviously given her something to make her sleep do you think? And you Alfred saying it looked that way. At least she won't be in pain while she's sleeping.'

Alfred took hold of my hand. 'Take it easy Ruth; don't talk if it's bothering you love.'

'No Alfred, I'm okay.'

'Anyway Ruth, Jonathon's sleeping at Auntie Lizzie's. Oh, and she sends you her love. She also said that she's finding it more difficult to walk now, and she'd much rather be at home and look after Jonathon. She said as long as we let her know how you are and to tell you she's thinking about you, but she can't bear to think of you lying in a hospital bed.'

'She is sweet. Last night I heard you say Mary, I'll kill him! And I thought please don't tell Alfred who did it, not tonight?'

Alfred laughed slightly, 'I would have killed him if I could have got my hands on him last night but anyway the police have him now.' Alfred spoke softly and I knew he really meant it. Last night I heard him sobbing at the side of my bed. Mary told me later that she didn't dare tell him who had done this to me for fear of what he would do in his state of mind.

After a short time the nurse joined us. 'You must go home now. The poor girl has had a rough time and she needs the rest. You can always come back tomorrow.'

'Thank you sister.' Alfred slowly got up and made for the door followed by Mary and the nurse.

'You both look as if you need some rest too. Don't worry, she'll be fine. We'll look after her, I promise.'

Mary told me Alfred drove her home. Jonathon was in bed and Auntie Lizzie had stayed up waiting for their return and asked after me so I told her you would be fine.

None of them slept much that night they tell me, and I only slept when a nurse gave me something to make me. When I was awake I could see my Uncle George's evil face and it made me break out in a sweat.

Early the following morning, it seems that Mary walked round to the police station and spoke to the desk sergeant before she returned to the hospital but he couldn't or wouldn't tell her much. On her way out of the station she saw the constable from the previous night so she stopped him and asked him what happened as she wasn't getting much information at all? He said he'd tell her but she mustn't tell a soul.

When she came to see me again she couldn't wait to give me the news.

'Well, the constable said that George Lewis's latest girl friend was brought in for questioning and she made a statement. She said she called to see why George wasn't at the inn like he said he would be. After looking through the window of his house and seeing him and you on the floor, the woman demanded George came to the door. It was then she saw the blood on his shirt. After that she decided to go away and call the police. The constable also said that he didn't know whether she suspected he'd committed a crime or whether it was sour grapes because she thought he had another girl friend. At least whatever it was, she did the right thing.

Ruth said, 'I owe her a lot. When you think what could have happened,'

Mary shivered. 'I think he's gone too far this time. He'll be going to court for attempted murder and ravishing you'

'Did he ravish me?'

'That's what he's being accused of.'

'Oh my God!'

The police came to question me as soon as they dared and I told them the full story including my suspicions of the murder at Fothergale Mansion. There were some thing's I missed out. In my heart I couldn't tell a soul that Jonathon was not Billy's child but Uncle George's and I did hope that my Uncle George didn't tell anyone either. I also hoped that my Uncle hadn't given me another pregnancy because the police told me that he'd taken advantage of me when I was unconscious.

Mary asked me a lot of questions about Uncle George and why I'd gone to see him on my own. My excuses were feeble but I made them up the best I could. I never wanted to reveal my secret. Alfred was very good. He didn't bombard me with questions. I knew he couldn't understand what I was doing at Uncle George's house but he didn't ask me.

The murder at Fothergale Mansion was investigated by the police. After making enquiries they found a maid who worked there when it happened and she gave evidence. There must have been a lot of blood and that's why Uncle George's shirt and scarf were in the parcel along with the other things. When the police broke into Uncle George's house and found the knife, it was engraved with the name of the mistress of the big house so George couldn't deny it.

'I knew he was bad I but I never realised how bad until now,' Mary was upset. 'And to think that he's my uncle, the same blood, it's unbelievable.'

It was a long drawn out affair with identity and court case and I was at court accompanied by Alfred all the time. Uncle George looked for me and when I gave evidence about the attack I could feel his eyes boring into me. It was degrading and I loathed doing it but it had to be done. When I stepped down I looked over to him and he gave me a knowing smirk. I hated him in that moment.

The maid gave evidence. She said she worked there at the time of the murder and now admitted that Uncle George had charmed her into letting him in secretly where she hid him in her bedroom. As soon as she left him on his own he slipped out and went into Lady Fothergale's bedroom where he took the jewellery. When he crept into the study and began to stuff things into his pocket, the master disturbed him. By this time, Uncle George held the master's paper knife in his hand and after a scuffle he plunged it into the master's heart. It seems that someone once bought the owners of the big house two paper knives, one each for the master and mistress of the house and had their names engraved on them both. Billy's friends also gave evidence about the find in the river. It brought it all back to me when Billy's name was mentioned and the tears began to run down my cheeks but Alfred squeezed my hand to support me.

When the judge put on the Black cap to sentence my Uncle George, we knew what his sentence was going to be before the judge uttered the words.

'You will be hanged...' I fainted.

Alfred carried me out of the court room and sat me down on a bench in the corridor. I began to come round and sobbed into his shoulder. Not a nice thought for my son to have a murderer for his father but at least he would never know. I would keep that secret to the grave.

When the day came for George to hang, I sat quietly and alone, I preferred it that way. I watched the clock, each minute, each second ticking slowly by. He was a bad man and deserved all he got really but he was my son's father and I would never forget that. It was instilled in my mind. But after all, he did keep our secret at the end. When the clock struck the hour I quietly sobbed. Later I called on Mary.

'I know you're upset about Uncle George,' Mary attempted to sympathise, 'but you know when you think about it, he was my uncle but he wasn't yours really, not by blood.' Mary thought for a while before she continued. 'I suppose I should be more upset than you but...I never liked him anyway.' I still didn't have anything to say so Mary carried on. 'I didn't know him as well as you did...thank goodness.'

My thoughts were my own but I knew that if Mary had only known how well I knew Uncle George she would be appalled. Alfred, Peter, Mary and Auntie Lizzie were always there for me and through them I managed to get through it all. Luckily, I didn't become pregnant from Uncle George's last attack. More than likely the whole ordeal wouldn't allow it, but I still had a child to bring up and I would see to it that he wouldn't suffer.

Mary saw much more of Peter after that. She would talk it over with me and ask my advice on occasions. He would go to her house at week-end for his Sunday lunch and stay there all day. I told her I couldn't think of a reason now why he shouldn't. Four evenings out of the six, Peter would go home with Mary after we closed the shop and Auntie Lizzie would have a meal ready for them. If she didn't because she wasn't well, then they would prepare a meal together. Mary would ask me how to make certain dishes and I would tell her. She said she wanted to look efficient. He would on occasion take Mary to the pictures or theatre and sometimes they would stay in the house and he would try, as it could get noisy with the Harrop children, to read the paper while she did the mending. Mary told me he was very patient as he loved children. The other two evenings, Peter would go home alone, and he eventually gave up the tennis and bowls. After a while, he proposed.

'I'm not going to say not yet Peter because I know what happened last time but you've put me in an awkward position.'

'I'm not going to go and ask someone else to marry me, I learned my lesson, so I'll be very patient this time and wait until you're ready as long as you will promise to marry me.'

'I will but at present there's Auntie Lizzie to think about.'

Auntie Lizzie weakened quickly after my distressing episode. It had been such a shock for her. I felt glad that the woman would never know the whole truth. Life seemed to get harder and harder all the time. Auntie Lizzie needed care so it was a blessing when Jonathon went back to school. Now I could help Mary to look after our Auntie.

When Peter came to see Mary the next time, she said they talked about Hannah.

He told her that Hannah was a good wife and he had missed her especially before he started going with Mary. Mary had worried about him when Hannah had consumption. She sometimes told me how terrified she was of Peter catching it. Then she told me the secret they had kept hidden of Hannah having a miscarriage. It was only after that, that Peter found out Hannah didn't want children. It was never mentioned and he had taken it for granted that she would. They stopped sharing a bed after that as she wanted to be sure. It was so sad. Peter guessed that Hannah had even forced the miscarriage but wasn't sure so he couldn't say anything.

Mary said that Peter told her he was happy enough with Hannah but Mary thought he was just putting on a brave face.

Ruth nodded. 'Hannah was a lovely girl. I think he could have done much worse, don't you Mary?'

'Yes, and he did say they had some happy times before everything went wrong.'

Peter and Mary waited for a while then finally decided to marry. They had a lovely wedding in Manchester and Mary looked so beautiful and pretty with her dark hair and long lashes that were just like her Dad's, a family trend. Mary insisted on a white wedding as it was her first and they found a vicar that was willing to oblige. The dress she made herself with a hat to match. She placed flowers half way round the brim and it looked stunning. It was a fantastic hat! Then Peter took Mary away for their honeymoon to an undisclosed place while Auntie Lizzie stayed with me then I could look after her.

Alfred came often and took Jonathon off my hands to give me a break. He took him to the park and the pictures and Jonathon loved it.

'Is he my Dad now mam?' Jonathon asked one evening when I put him to bed.

'No love but he's as good as. I don't think you could get a better one.'

'Can I call him dad?'

'No Jonathon. Maybe one day but not yet.' I didn't tell Alfred what Jonathon had said but I did think about it a lot.

When Mary and Peter returned from their honeymoon, I couldn't wait to find out where they had been and Mary was only too willing to tell me all about it.

'It was wonderful Ruth. Peter took me in a boat.'

'That must have been lovely,' I said eagerly.

'It was. He didn't even tell me where we were going. When we were in the middle of the sea, it was wonderful, we were nowhere near land. To think there was nothing beneath us either…except water. It was wonderful.'

I noticed she said wonderful rather a lot.

'Where did you go?' I asked.

He took me all the way to the Isle of Man to a town called…what was it called Peter?'

'Onchan, darling.'

'That's it; it's funny how you can forget. This big boat, well, I've never been in one before. It was…'

'Wonderful?' I asked.

'It was wonderful. Wasn't it darling,' Mary said turning to Peter.

I laughed. It was good to see Mary so happy and I thought again about what Jonathon said. If this is what marriage did for you then maybe it would be worth considering soon.

'Anyway,' said Mary, 'Peter and I have discussed Auntie Lizzie and we thought it was a good idea if she came to live with us at Peter's house. What do you think about that Auntie?'

Auntie Lizzie pondered about that. 'Am I such a nuisance that I'm under discussion?'

'You're not a nuisance Auntie Lizzie. I want you for selfish reasons.'

'What are those,' asked Lizzie.

'I know you're not very strong but you can cook and I thought that maybe you could, only if you feel like it of course, prepare a meal for us sometimes. It would be such a help.'

Auntie Lizzie looked from one to the other and nodded her head. 'As long as I won't be in the way.'

'Never…you won't ever be in the way Auntie.' Mary got up and went over to Auntie Lizzie to plant a kiss on her cheek.

'Are you sure Peter?' Auntie Lizzie asked.

'Very sure. If that's what my wife wants then it's okay with me. Besides, we both love you very much.' Peter went over to her and gave her a hug. 'You are family after all.'

Auntie Lizzie moved in with them and the Harrop's applied to the town hall for the tenancy of Mary's house, after asking Mary's permission, and it was accepted which was a good thing as Mrs. Harrop was pregnant again.

Occasionally, Auntie Lizzie prepared a meal for when Peter and Mary came home from work. When I called on them sometimes, they appeared to be happy and contented. Peter and Mary's business thrived and they employed more staff.

I started working for Alfred on a part-time basis, feeding paper into the printing machines and the machine that put lines on the paper, numbering pages and sometimes using the guillotine to cut the paper to size. Alfred proposed again but I still found that I couldn't say yes, I knew I should as there had been a time when I really thought I would but somehow I couldn't do it.

I think he's a lovely man Ruth,' Auntie Lizzie commented one day, 'and I think he'll make a good father for Jonathon. You've been very lucky finding two such men. Some women have trouble finding one.'

The next Christmas we all got together at Peter and Mary's to swap presents. We missed Uncle Jim at the piano but instead played games with Jonathon. It was one way of keeping all the family together. Through it all we found Peter and Mary in very high spirits. Later, Peter announced, once he filled everyone's glass, that Mary was expecting a baby the following June. We all raised our glass.

'Congratulations to both of you,' we said in unison.

I watched them together. They looked so proud. It took time for them to finally marry but they got there in the end. It was a shame about Hannah though. After their meal we all went to her grave and as Peter laid flowers he whispered. 'We're expecting a baby in June Hannah. It's our first and we're very happy about it but you'll always have your place in my heart.'

'I know she'll be happy for me,' he said as he looked at Mary and she wiped the tears from his eyes.

After, me, Alfred and Jonathon walked round to Billy's grave. I laid the flowers and Alfred and Jonathon walked off and left me to grieve alone.

'Oh Billy, I still wear your locket around my neck as I promised I would, even though I'm with Alfred now. He knows, he's a good man and he doesn't mind. I've tried very hard to understand why you left me like you did but I never will. I don't think you ever really knew how much…how deep my love was for you. Maybe one day I'll forgive you but it's very difficult.'

Auntie Lizzie's health deteriorated but after much thought Peter paid for someone to help to look after her then Mary could have a few hours a week at the shop. It would be a break for her and keep her hand in with the business. Her organisation skills along with her millinery and dressmaking made them the 'in' place to buy for women. Their business continued to thrive with Mary's input and she worked up to the week before giving birth. I helped whenever I could.

Me and Alfred made part of the business into a shop and sold a selection of stationery goods which boosted the profits and I enjoyed working behind the counter.

When Mary started in labour, I was by her side along with the midwife. Peter stayed at home, leaving the shop to the staff to run, although he wasn't much help at home. After three days of labour the baby was delivered by forceps. We were thrilled to discover it was a daughter, Barbara, weighing eight pounds three ounces and she was beautiful. Poor Mary needed stitches, performed by the doctor and had to take it easy for a while.

The baby's health wasn't good at first but she soon improved. I smiled as I watched the loving parents with their offspring and thought how different Jonathon's birth had been.

The plan was for me to bring Jonathon with me while I stayed with Mary, to help her through the first two weeks with the baby. Auntie Lizzie's health deteriorated and she took to her bed so I was kept busy for longer. Mary's health improved and she soon went into a routine. Peter helped with the washing and ironing, even learning to cook good substantial meals to keep Mary healthy while I fed the baby.

A month later Lizzie died; it was as though she waited to see the baby before she gave up on life.

At her funeral, we all stood by the graveside and I went over in my mind all that happened over the years. How things fell into place as though life was all planned. I realised that this was the end of an era and a new beginning had started with Jonathon and Barbara. Life changed so much over time and who could tell how many more changes there were to be in the future.

When Jonathon started to call Alfred 'dad,' I didn't complain, much to the surprise of Mary. As Billy wasn't Jonathon's dad there was no need to raise objections. Mary didn't know that so she couldn't possibly understand but she didn't say anything anyway and I would never tell.

A month later Alfred proposed again but this last proposal sounded a little different than the others.

'I insist on marrying you and won't take no for an answer. You've looked after everyone else. Now you need someone to look after you and Jonathon, and *I'm* going to do it—it's my job,' so I eventually agreed and we arranged a date.

Our wedding was a little quieter than Mary's. Jonathon was present and looked very smart in his suit. I wore a blue suit with hat to match, made at Kershaw's, and Alfred looked really, really proud as he took my hand and pushed it through his arm.

'Mine at last,' he murmured in my ear.

We honeymooned in Blackpool while Jonathon stayed at home this time with Mary and Peter. Alfred took me in the tower ballroom and I learned how to dance the Charleston. I thoroughly enjoyed those days in Blackpool with Alfred and he taught me how to love again. I owe him such a lot.

On our way home in the car I gazed into space, my thoughts going back to the day of the fire. My little brothers, my Step-Dad and how he'd come home drunk. How my Mam defended me when my stepfather lost his temper and began to beat me. Later, when he lit the candle and went upstairs to bed.

Then the fire…

And when I awoke…

But those were yesterday's tomorrows.

~The End~